TWO CROWNS, TWO ISLANDS, ONE LEGACY

*A royal family torn apart
by pride and its lust for power,
reunited by purity and passion*

The islands of Adamas have been torn into two rival kingdoms:

TWO CROWNS
The Stefani diamond has been split
as a symbol of their feud.

TWO ISLANDS
Gorgeous Greek princes reign supreme
over glamorous Aristo.
Smoldering sheikhs rule
the desert island of Calista.

ONE LEGACY
Whoever reunites the diamonds will rule all.

THE ROYAL HOUSE OF KAREDES

Many years ago there were two islands ruled as one kingdom—Adamas. But bitter family feuds and rivalry caused the kingdom to be ripped in two. The islands were ruled separately, as Aristo and Calista, and the infamous Stefani coronation diamond was split as a symbol of the feud, and placed in the two new crowns.

But when the king divided the islands between his son and daughter, he left them with these words:

"You will rule each island for the good of the people and bring out the best in your kingdom. But my wish is that eventually these two jewels, like the islands, will be reunited. Aristo and Calista are more successful, more beautiful and more powerful as one nation—Adamas."

Now King Aegeus Karedes of Aristo is dead, and the island's coronation diamond is missing! The Aristans will stop at nothing to get it back, but the ruthless sheikh king of Calista is hot on their heels.

Whether by seduction, blackmail or marriage, the jewel must be found. As the stories unfold, secrets and sins from the past are revealed, and desire, love and passion war with royal duty. But who will discover in time that it is innocence of body and purity of heart that can unite the islands of Adamas once again?

Marion Lennox

THE PRINCE'S CAPTIVE WIFE

THE ROYAL HOUSE *of* KAREDES

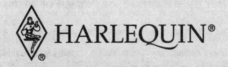

HARLEQUIN®

TORONTO • NEW YORK • LONDON
AMSTERDAM • PARIS • SYDNEY • HAMBURG
STOCKHOLM • ATHENS • TOKYO • MILAN • MADRID
PRAGUE • WARSAW • BUDAPEST • AUCKLAND

With thanks to my fabulous coauthors,
whose writing has made this series sizzle.

Recycling programs
for this product may
not exist in your area.

ISBN-13: 978-0-373-12851-8

THE PRINCE'S CAPTIVE WIFE

First North American Publication 2009.

Copyright © 2009 by Harlequin Books S.A.

Special thanks and acknowledgment are given to Marion Lennox for her
contribution to *The Royal House of Karedes* series.

www.eHarlequin.com

Printed in U.S.A.

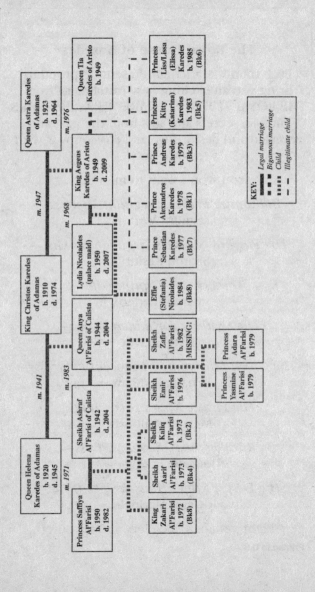

The Royal House of Karedes

Each month, Harlequin Presents is proud to bring you an exciting new installment from THE ROYAL HOUSE OF KAREDES. As the stories unfold, secrets and sins from the past are revealed and desire, love and passion war with royal duty!

You won't want to miss out!

Billionaire Prince, Pregnant Mistress—
Sandra Marton

The Playboy Sheikh's Virgin Stable-Girl—
Sharon Kendrick

The Prince's Captive Wife—
Marion Lennox

The Sheikh's Forbidden Virgin—
Kate Hewitt

The Greek Billionaire's Innocent Princess—
Chantelle Shaw

The Future-King's Love-Child—
Melanie Milburne

Ruthless Boss, Royal Mistress—
Natalie Anderson

The Desert King's Housekeeper Bride—
Carol Marinelli

Eight volumes to collect and treasure!

CHAPTER ONE

'SHE was only seventeen?'

'We're talking ten years ago. I was barely out of my teens myself.'

'Does that make a difference?' The uncrowned king of Aristo stared across his massive desk at his brother, his aquiline face dark with fury. 'Have we not had enough scandal?'

'Not of my making.' Prince Andreas Christos Karedes, third in line to the Crown of Aristo, stood his ground against his older brother with the disdain he always used in this family of testosterone-driven males. His brothers might be acknowledged womanizers, but Andreas made sure his affairs were discreet.

'Until now,' Sebastian said. 'Not counting your singularly spectacular divorce, which had a massive impact. But this is worse. You need to sort it before it explodes over all of us.'

'How the hell can I sort it?'

'Get rid of her.'

'You're not saying…'

Sebastian shook his head, obviously rejecting the idea—though a tinge of regret in his voice said the option wasn't altogether unattractive.

And Andreas even sympathized. Since their father's death, all three brothers had been dragged through the mire of the media spotlight, and the political unrest was threatening to destroy them. In their thirties, impossibly handsome, wealthy beyond belief, indulged and fêted, the brothers were now facing realities they had no idea what to do with.

'Though if I was our father...' Sebastian added and Andreas shuddered. Who knew what the old king would have done if he'd discovered Holly's secret? Thank God he'd never found out. Not that King Aegeus could have taken the moral high ground. His father's past actions had got them into this mess.

'You'll make a better king than our father ever was,' Andreas said softly. 'What filthy dealing made him dispose of the royal diamond?'

'That's my concern,' Sebastian said. There could be no royal coronation until the diamond was found—they all knew that—but the way the media was baying for blood there might not be a coronation even then. Without the diamond the rules had changed. If any more scandals broke... 'This girl...'

'Holly.'

'You remember her?'

'Of course I remember her.'

'Then she'll be easy to find. We'll buy her off—do whatever it takes, but she mustn't talk to anyone.'

'If she wanted to make a scandal she could have done it years ago.'

'So it's been simmering in the wings for years. To have it surface now...' Sebastian rose and fixed Andreas with a look that was almost as deadly as the one used by the old king. 'It can't happen, brother. We have to make sure she's not in a position to bring us down.'

'I'll contact her.'

'You'll go nowhere near her until we're sure of her reaction. Not even a phone call. For all we know her phones are already tapped. I'll have her brought here.'

'I can arrange...'

'You stay right out of it until she's on our soil. You're heading the corruption inquiry. With Alex still on his honeymoon—of all the times for our brother to demand to marry, this must surely be the worst—I need you more than ever. If you leave now and this leaks, we can almost guarantee losing the crown.'

'So how do you propose to persuade her to come?'

'Oh, I'll persuade her,' Sebastian said grimly. 'She's only a slip of a girl. She might be your past, but there's no way she's messing with our future.'

It was time to leave, but of all the places Holly had to farewell, this was the hardest.

The grave was tiny—a simple stone plaque nestled under the shade of the vast river-red-gum that gave this Australian cattle station its name. The tree was ancient. The native Australians who'd lived here for generations called it Munwannay—resting place—and when Holly's tiny son had died it had seemed the only place to let him lie.

How could she walk away?

How could she walk away from any of this? Holly sank to her knees before her son's grave and turned to gaze back over the homestead—the rambling, old house with its wide verandas, its French windows opening the house to every breeze, the neglected garden she'd loved so much since she was a little girl.

Andreas had loved this garden.

Andreas had loved everything about this place. And she'd loved Andreas.

Well, that was another thing she needed to walk away from. The memory of Prince Andreas Karedes. He'd been twenty when he'd come here to spend six months experiencing life in Australia's remote outback. She'd been seventeen.

She was twenty-seven now. It was more than time that she move on—from this place, as well as a love that had been doomed from the start.

She'd been stalling for as long as possible, trying to keep the property presentable in case new owners could be found, but it had been on the market since her father's death six months ago. Financially it was impossible to keep going, and it was becoming bleaker every day as she watched it deteriorate. Finally she'd transferred her job—teaching on the School of the Air—to the educational base at Alice Springs. This was the end.

She touched her baby's gravestone one last time, aching with regret and loss. And then she paused, looking upward as the stillness of the hot April morning was shattered.

A helicopter was arrowing in fast from the east. It was big and powerful, a much larger machine than those owned by the larger local landowners. All black, almost menacing, it swept in low across the bare paddocks, heading straight for the homestead.

Holly winced. There'd been a trickle of potential buyers looking at the place since it had gone on the market. No one had been interested. Munwannay needed a massive injection of cash and enthusiasm to build it up to the magnificent property it had once been. If these were more potential buyers sent by the rural land agents, they'd react the same as the others. They'd walk through the faded splendour of the old homestead; they'd look at the weathered outbuildings and the dilapidated infrastructure and they'd walk away. If these buyers were coming in such a helicopter they'd have more money than most, but then they could afford to buy a more prestigious place.

And she didn't want them here now. Not on her last day.

But they were landing. She watched them as the chopper settled in a cloud of dust; as the doors opened. Four men in dark jeans and black T-shirts jumped out. Big men. Powerfully built, all of them.

Odd. Up until now potential buyers had been local farmers wanting to extend their own landholdings, distinctive by age and by weathering—or men in suits from the city.

No matter. She needed to be gracious. If this place sold it would give her a hope of settling the crippling debts left by her father's refusal to believe his circumstances in the world had changed. She pinned a smile on her face and hurried forward, not wanting them to come here—to see the tiny gravestone she loved so much.

They were young to be buyers, she thought as they approached. And foreign? They were olive skinned, as Andreas had been. They looked serious, purposeful, striding across the paddock towards her with an intent at odds with a potential buyer's initial appraisal.

A shiver of unease shot down her spine. She was alone here. Too alone.

She gave herself a swift mental shake. She was being fanciful. They'd hardly come here in such a helicopter with the intent to do her personal harm, and there was nothing left to steal.

She smoothed her suddenly damp palms on her jeans, tucked—or tried to tuck—her unruly blonde curls behind her ears, firmed her smile and called a greeting.

'Hi. Can I help you?'

There was no answering smile on any of their faces, and Holly's sense of unease deepened.

'Are you Holly Cavanagh?' the leading man called.

'I am.'

Maybe they were Greek, she thought. They had the same accent as Andreas. Maybe they were even from Aristo, the island country Andreas had come from.

That was being even more fanciful. Or maybe not. She'd read that ruthless dealings by the old King Aegeus had turned Aristo into an economic force to be reckoned with. There were casinos there now, easy money, rumours of corruption in high places. Maybe there were citizens with the money to transform a place like this.

Maybe Andreas had heard Munwannay was on the market, she thought suddenly. He'd loved it. Maybe…

Maybe she needed to stop thinking, for the men had reached her.

She stretched her hand out in greeting. The first man to

reach her took it, but not with the light, formal greeting she was expecting. His grip was harsh and unrelenting. She tugged back but he didn't release her.

'You need to come with us,' he said, and she stared at him in blank astonishment.

'I'm sorry?'

But he was already tugging her towards the helicopter. As she resisted one of the other men grasped her by the other arm. They had a hand under each elbow now and were almost lifting her; hauling her fast towards the helicopter.

She screamed.

There was no one to hear. Munwannay had been deserted long since by everyone but this slip of a girl, whose efforts to save the place had come to nothing.

'Get her into the chopper, fast,' the leader said, in a language she recognized; a language she'd learned for fun so she and Andreas could speak to each other without her parents understanding.

'No. No!' But she couldn't fight them. She was one woman among four men surely trained to use brute strength to good effect.

'Shut up,' one of the men snapped at her, and another hauled her forward so roughly he almost dislocated her arm.

'Don't hurt her,' another snapped, urgent. 'The prince said we're not to harm her.'

'What…? Why?' They were lifting her bodily into the chopper with as little trouble as if she'd been a bag of chaff.

'Just be quiet,' another of them said, quite kindly as if humouring a child. 'And there's no use in struggling. The Prince Andreas wants you, and what the Prince Andreas wants, the Prince Andreas gets.'

The call came just after dinner. The manservant beckoned Andreas discreetly from his family's presence, and he slipped silently away.

In truth the royal family of Karedes was so caught up with

the scandals rocking them right now, the absence of Andreas from their midst would hardly be missed. In his father's time it would have been unthinkable to leave the table before port was served to the males of the family, but the king was dead.

Long live the king, Andreas thought bleakly as he made his way swiftly from the room. All they needed was a coronation. And a diamond. And no more scandal.

In this atmosphere Holly's secret was enough to blast them off the throne.

At least the first part of Sebastian's plan had worked. He knew it the moment he picked up the phone. 'She's on her way,' Georgiou said, and he drew in his breath in relief. He hadn't thought it would be so easy.

In truth he didn't know what he'd thought. He'd expected Holly to be married by now. It had been a shock to hear she was still single.

That had been the least of his shocks.

And now she was on her way. To him.

'She agreed to come straight away? There was no argument?'

There was a silence on the end of the line and Andreas's jet-black brows snapped down. 'Why don't you answer?' he demanded as the silence lengthened.

'Our instructions were to use whatever means necessary to get her to you.'

'But you asked her to come? Your instructions were to tell her she was needed here urgently. To offer her every comfort…'

'And if she didn't agree, the Prince Sebastian told us to ignore her protests. She was alone. She was expecting the land agent. Our decision was that it was wisest to move fast. Discussion would have wasted time and maybe jeopardized our ability to take her at all.'

'So…'

'So we put her on the helicopter whether she willed it or not, then transferred her to a plane which took us up north and then on. There's no problem. There was no one to see us come or her go.'

He closed his eyes, appalled, the ramifications of what they'd done slamming home. 'You abducted her.'

'There was no choice,' Georgiou said firmly. 'She will not listen. All through the flight we've been trying to tell her you simply wish to see her, but the lady is too angry to listen. She bit Maris.'

'There was a struggle?'

'She didn't wish to come. Of course there was a struggle.'

His breath hissed with dismay. For them to abduct her… What the hell must she be thinking? And if this got out… A prince of the royal house of Karedes kidnapping an Australian woman; dragging her out of the country against her will…

'Did you hurt her?' he demanded, incredulous.

'We haven't hurt her,' Georgiou said, defensive. 'We have our orders. Though she fights like a wildcat'

'I don't care how she fights,' Andreas snapped, appalled at the results of Sebastian's curt orders. 'You will not retaliate. She's just a girl.'

'She's a woman,' Georgiou corrected him. 'She's every bit a woman. Mixed with tigress.'

Andreas thought back to the Holly he'd left ten years ago. Even at seventeen Holly had had spirit.

Years ago he'd spent a glorious six months on Holly's parents' property, experiencing life in the Australian outback before taking up his royal duties. It had been a dispensation granted reluctantly to a younger son by his father, the king. His relationship with Holly had flared from nowhere and turned to wildfire. The young Andreas had been desperate for it to continue, but Holly had been strong enough for both of them.

'You don't belong in my world and I don't belong in yours,' she'd said firmly as he'd held her close one last time and declared he couldn't leave her. 'You're needed at home. Your life is on Aristo. You're promised in marriage to a princess. Andreas, don't make it harder than it needs to be for both of us. Just go.'

So he'd gone, trying hard to block the stricken expression

he'd glimpsed on his beloved's face as Holly had turned away that one last time. Yes, there had been tears—he'd been close to them himself—but she was right. He was a royal prince, already promised in marriage. Holly had aging parents to care for and a budding career as a teacher on School of the Air. Holly and Andreas belonged on separate sides of the world.

So that had been it. He'd tried not to think of her for ten long years, through a tumultuous royal marriage that ended in acrimonious divorce, through his career as a royal prince with princely duties, through a life in the goldfish bowl of royalty. His was a life of service to the crown, a crown that must be protected at all costs.

A crown that Holly herself was now threatening to undermine, whether she knew it or not.

'Just bring her here fast,' he said, his tone becoming harsher as he recalled all that was at stake. 'Bring her straight to the palace.'

'There might be problems,' Georgiou said cautiously.

'What sort of problems?'

'I told you. She's not…quiet,' he said. 'There's no saying she won't scream her head off.'

'Why would she do that?'

Another silence. Georgiou obviously thought that was a stupid question.

Okay, maybe it was. If they'd dragged her here against her will… If she was still even slightly the Holly he knew…

'I'll meet you at the airport,' he said.

'Not the main landing strip,' Georgiou said urgently. 'You need to talk to the lady privately. If she'll talk to you.'

'She'll talk to me,' Andreas said grimly.

'Maybe,' Georgiou said. 'How long is it since you've seen her?'

'Ten years.'

'Then maybe she's changed,' Georgiou said and there was suddenly a note of admiration in his tone. 'Maybe this woman has learned to fight.'

'She could fight ten years ago.'

'Could you win then?' Georgiou asked diffidently. 'With respect, Your Majesty… It takes four strong men to hold her now. Will you be able to do it?'

They were landing.

Holly had long since stopped struggling. Once she'd been bundled ignominiously onto the jet and the jet was in the air she'd accepted that fighting was useless. She'd withdrawn into what she hoped was dignified silence.

Not that she felt the least bit dignified. She'd been wearing ancient jeans and a dust-stained shirt when she'd been grabbed. She'd just completed a last inspection of the bores and water troughs—for the sake of the kangaroos and emus on the place, for the cattle had been sold long ago—and her blonde curls were thick with dust. Twenty-four hours later that dust was still with her. She'd scrubbed her face in the airplane washroom but there was no make-up to disguise the shadows under her eyes. She looked grubby and exhausted and fearful.

Not fearful, she thought savagely. She was damned if she'd show these louts fear.

Maybe it wasn't these men she had to fear. Andreas wanted her. Andreas had taken her, whether she agreed or not.

Ten years ago she would have agreed. Ten years ago if Andreas had said come she'd have followed him to the ends of the earth. She'd fallen so deeply in love that she'd given everything she had. She would have given more.

Then she'd been wild, passionate, desperate to find a life outside the confines of her parents' farm. Andreas had blasted into her dreary life, tall, dark and mysterious, a royal prince, twenty to her seventeen, laughing, imperious, seemingly as eager to be a part of her world as she'd been to be part of his. Of course they'd fallen in love.

She'd thought later, in the bleak aftermath of loss, that maybe that was why her parents had arranged to host Andreas. They'd known two young things might be drawn together as they had been. Her parents had had illusions of grandeur, and offering to host a young prince on a farm-stay when they had such a young, impressionable daughter was surely dangerous.

Maybe they'd had a royal marriage in mind. Who knew? All she knew was that her parents had achieved more than they'd bargained for.

A daughter desolate.

A tiny grandson, unacknowledged by his father. Now dead.

Don't think of Adam, she told herself fiercely as the plane started to descend. Don't you dare cry.

She blinked and stared fixedly out the plane window. They were circling the Adamas kingdom now. Home of Andreas.

Adamas consisted of two vast islands, the glamorous Aristo and the desert lands of Calista. Andreas had told her so much of these islands that she felt she knew them already. They were once one kingdom, ruled by the Royal House of Karedes, but now split acrimoniously into two by a warring brother and sister.

Andreas's father ruled Aristo, and Andreas helped rule, as one of three royal sons. Andreas was married. She knew that much. The wedding had taken place soon after he'd returned from Australia. The story of the ceremony's magnificence had even reached the women's magazines in the Munwannay General Store. She'd read of it and wept. After that she'd studiously avoided any mention of him, but he was probably saddled with a tribe of royal children by now.

Why had he hauled her here?

Maybe he was bored in his marriage, she thought. The idea had crept into her mind as the flight wore on, a vicious stab of unwanted imagination. Andreas had been married for over nine years now. Nine years was time enough to tire of a wife, especially a wife who'd been arranged for him in the first place. Maybe he was thinking back to the wild, tumultuous passion that had sent them past the bounds of care.

Surely he wouldn't think…

Why else would he want her?

She curled her fingers so tightly into her palms that her nails cut into her skin. Surely in this day and age he wouldn't dare. And if he thought she would…

But… Andreas, she thought. Andreas, Andreas.

See, there was the trouble. Andreas had moved on. He'd lived another life, whereas she'd been stuck in a time warp, trying to hold the farm together for her father's sake. Trying to forge a career for herself, while never being able to leave one tiny grave.

And never being able to forget Andreas.

Andreas was down there. Prince Andreas Christos Karedes of Aristo. A royal prince, waiting for her.

She dug her fingernails even deeper into her palms. What did he want of her?

He could have nothing. Nothing! What was between them was over. She just had to get away from these thugs and she'd find some way to leave.

But she'd see Andreas first.

The plane didn't taxi towards the airport buildings but instead stopped far out on the runway.

Andreas drove himself out to meet it. He didn't need Sebastian to tell him that the fewer people who saw this first reunion, the better. He'd like to get rid of Holly's minders and the aircrew first, but that was impossible. They'd have to be paid well for their silence.

He reached the plane and waited with ill-concealed impatience for the steps to be put in place and the doors to open.

Georgiou emerged first. The big man stopped on the top step and looked helplessly down at Andreas. He held up his hands, as if in surrender.

'You want us to carry the cargo down?' he asked, with a wary glance at the airport workers within earshot. 'She…we could have trouble.'

'You and your men leave the plane,' Andreas said grimly. 'I'll come up.'

'You'll be…safe?'

'Don't be ridiculous,' he snapped, and climbed the steps with purpose. This was getting farcical. Even though he hated the idea that she'd been abducted, he needed to remind himself that this woman had deceived him. She was here because of that deceit. He had every reason to be angry and the sooner he had it out with her, the better.

Or maybe there was some simple explanation. Maybe this could be a five-minute conversation and she could leave again. It could all be a mistake.

Maybe.

'She's up the back. She's hardly spoken to us since we left Australia, and only then in anger,' Georgiou said, standing aside, and Andreas nodded and entered the cabin. And saw her.

For a moment his world stood still.

Holly.

She was just the same. His Holly. The Holly he'd held in his heart all these years. Holly, in her tattered jeans and T-shirt, her hair wild and tumbled, always laughing, always teasing. The image he'd loved most was of her riding bareback across the paddocks, daring him to keep up with her if he could.

Lovely Holly, with her beautiful body. Her bright, sapphire-blue eyes, her fierce intelligence, her low, throaty chuckle…

She wasn't chuckling now. Her face looked set and grim. Her arms were crossed firmly across her breasts as she sat where she'd clearly sat for the entire journey. She looked dishevelled and weary and very, very angry. She met his gaze and it was almost a physical jolt. A stormy tempest about to break.

'Holly,' he said, and maybe he even said it tenderly before he could help himself, but the tenderness stopped right there.

'How dare you?' she snapped and, as he took a step towards her, she rose and moved out into the aisle.

'I wished to see you,' he said and her eyes flashed fire.

'You're seeing me. Your thugs dragged me into their helicopter without a word. They brought me here with no explanation. Your thugs. That's what they are, Andreas, and so are you for employing them. A stupid, cowardly thug to set four men on a defenceless woman.'

'You're not defenceless,' he said, taking a further step toward her and feeling the faint tug of a smile at the corners of his eyes. 'You bit Maris.'

'So I did.' If looks could kill he'd be stabbed to the heart. 'I wish I'd bitten him harder, but then I'd probably catch something vile. You're pond scum, the lot of you. Why have you dragged me here?'

'There are things we need to talk about,' he said, forcing his tone to mildness.

'So use the phone.'

'That wouldn't have been wise,' he said and took another step forward and maybe that was a mistake. For her hand came up and slapped, a solid, ringing slap that pushed his face aside and echoed around and around the confines of the cabin. He gasped, his face darkening in anger. Instinctively his hand came up and caught her wrist, dragging it down.

'Don't you touch me,' she snapped and lashed out with her feet. Her leather boot hit his shin and it was all he could do not to yelp.

'Do you know what the penalties are for assaulting royalty?' he demanded, astounded, moving adroitly so she was held out of kicking range.

'Do you know what the penalties are for international kidnap?' she countered, still trying to kick. 'For grabbing me and hauling me here against my will? I don't know what you want with me, Andreas Karedes. Tell your thugs to turn the plane round and take me home.'

She wrenched her wrists so hard he released them. She staggered back. His hands came out and caught her shoulders. She steadied and her hand came up and slapped again. Harder.

Ouch. If he wasn't careful he'd have a black eye to explain to the press.

'I just want an explanation...' he started, but she was too angry to let him go on.

'I don't care what you want. Let me go.'

'Not until you tell me what I need to know.'

'You can't do this.'

'Holly, it seems I already have,' he said wearily. 'I'm sorry you were abducted. I meant to persuade you to come—not to coerce you. But now you're here, you need to accept the royal imperative. You'll stay until we have an explanation.'

Um…maybe that hadn't worked. As an apology for what had happened, maybe it lacked a certain finesse. Holly certainly seemed to think so.

She stared at him blindly, two spots of flame high on her cheeks revealing that her temper had her right out of control. She glanced out the window. There was a cluster of airport workers in sight, clearly waiting to do the plane's routine maintenance, or at least assist it to leave the runway it was blocking.

'Aristo is a civilized country,' she said, suddenly thoughtful, almost civil.

'What…?'

'You have laws,' she continued. 'Laws that even include kidnapping, I believe. Royalty may have been able to rape and pillage in the past, but I'd imagine those days are well and truly over.'

'What I say, goes,' he snapped, startled.

'Does it? I wonder?' She eyed him thoughtfully. She closed her eyes—and she screamed.

It was a scream to end all screams. It was a scream perfected years ago by a lonely child who'd had a taste for dramatics and miles of open space to practise. It was a scream that had every head within two hundred yards of the plane swivelling to see what was happening.

He grabbed her and hauled her towards him, reaching for her mouth. She elbowed him in the ribs and kept right on screaming.

His fingers closed on her mouth.

She bit. Hard.

Andreas swore, then strode across to haul the door closed, giving them a measure of privacy. Just in time, for Holly had taken a breath and was opening her mouth to scream again.

'I wouldn't bother,' he said, staring down incredulously at the small teeth marks on his palm. That she could do such a thing... 'You'll not be heard through the doors.'

'I demand the police,' she spat. 'I want the consulate. You can't do this.'

'This is Aristo and I'm the royal family,' he said. 'I can do what I want.'

'Not with me you can't.'

And then Georgiou was back, shoving his way urgently through the aircraft door and staring at his boss's hand in incredulity. 'You're bleeding.'

'It's nothing.'

'I hope he gets rabies and dies,' Holly hissed.

'So he might, being bitten by a mad—'

'Leave it,' Andreas snapped. 'You'll have to take her to Eueilos.'

'Sir, she's out of control,' Georgiou said urgently. 'There's no one on Eueilos except Sophia and Nikos, and they're too old to defend you.'

'I'll tell them to lock up the firearms,' Andreas said dryly. 'She won't hurt one elderly couple who have nothing to do with this, and there's no way she can get away from the island.' He glanced at his watch. 'I can't stay. I need to face parliament in an hour and if I'm not there, there'll be questions.'

Georgiou gave a wry smile. 'Very good,' he murmured. 'But can we keep this one under wraps?'

'I'm not staying under any wraps,' Holly hissed, kicking backward at him. 'Andreas, what the hell do you think you're doing?'

What was he doing? He thought of the report lying on his desk at home and his face hardened. She was threatening everything. One secret, which surely he'd had the right to know...even before his marriage?

But she'd gone past the point of hysterical.

'I'm protecting my own,' he said at last. 'I have no idea what happened to you after I left Australia, but it's threatening the future of this country. I'm sorry it's had to come to this, Holly, but I want the truth. You'll go to Eueilos and you'll await my pleasure. I'll see you when I'm ready.'

CHAPTER TWO

IT WAS four days before he could leave. The corruption enquiry was reaching its zenith and, as head of the investigative committee, Andreas had to work through the mess of corrupt officialdom while trying to figure when he could get to Eueilos.

Maybe Holly would be better off with time to calm down, he decided, but only he knew how hard it was to concentrate on the issues at hand. When he finally left it was with a sense of relief—but also apprehension.

The island of Eueilos, an idyllic hideaway given to him on his coming of age by his father, King Aegeus, had long been his refuge. From childhood, Andreas had shown a distaste for the pomp and splendour of royalty. He was caught in the royal web. To walk away was an impossibility instilled in him from birth, but Eueilos was his. His wife had never liked it. Christina had loved the bright lights of the city, and even the capital of Aristo was too quiet for her, so he'd always been free to do with his island as he wished.

He'd built a pavilion—a whim, fashioned on the desert tents used by his royal cousins on the neighbouring island of Calista. From a distance it looked like a series of vast marquees, joined together in a circle. As a visitor grew closer he'd realize the 'tents' were in fact made from whitewashed timber panels. Every wall could be drawn back, opening almost the entire pavilion to the sea breezes that blew softly all year round.

In the centre of the pavilion, exposed when the walls were drawn back, was a vast swimming pool, large enough to classify as a lagoon. The island's beaches were wide and golden, the sea always inviting, so the swimming pool was pure luxury, for when one was simply too lazy to walk the hundred yards or so to the shore.

He came as often as he could, when the demands and public spotlight of royalty became overpowering. He had a discreet couple as housekeeper and groundsman, and that was his total staff.

He loved it, as once he'd fallen for Holly's home, he thought as his plane came in to land. He was flying himself—a small Cessna he'd learned to fly on Holly's farm. Holly herself had taught him the rudiments, and every time he flew he...

No. He didn't think of her. Hell, he'd been married, divorced—so much had happened since he'd last seen her.

He was about to see her now.

His hand came up to touch his face in remembrance. His dark skin didn't show a bruise, but he still felt the imprint of her slap. Had she calmed down yet?

She must have calmed down sufficiently to answer his questions. There was no choice. He was here to stay until his questions were answered.

And until Sebastian's outrageous suggestion was dealt with?

Sophia, his housekeeper, met him at the entrance to the pavilion. She'd been baking, and the smell of baklava assailed his senses, making him smile as this place always did. Sophia had been his nanny until he was ten. When he'd been granted the island he'd gone to find her. She and her husband, Nikos, ran this place and their comfortable presence always had the capacity to make his cares seem less.

But: 'She's not here,' Sophia said and his cares came flooding back.

'What?'

'She's at the beach on the far side of the island,' Sophia told him, watching his face. 'It's the furthest place from this house. Georgiou told her you would come. She says to tell you not to bother, unless it's to arrange her flight away from here.' She frowned at him. 'Andreas, this woman…Holly… she is very angry.'

'Not as angry as I am,' Andreas said grimly.

'I didn't raise you to take revenge on women,' Sophia said, and folded her arms across her bosom and glared up at him. She was five feet nothing compared to his six feet one, but height was nothing. She'd box his ears if she thought it necessary, he thought ruefully. Of all the people in his life, Sophia was the only one who didn't treat him as a royal prince. Rather she treated him as a boy, to be indulged but also to be brought into line as necessary.

'She's a good girl,' Sophia added, still aggressive. 'And she's frightened. I've told her there's nothing to be frightened of while I'm on this island. I don't know why you've brought her here, Your Majesty, but you touch her and you'll answer to me.'

Sophia only ever called him Your Majesty when she was in the presence of others—or was really troubled. Andreas forced a smile to reassure her.

'I won't hurt her.'

'You already have. There are bruises on her wrists.'

'That wasn't me.'

'It was Georgiou and that's the same thing.'

'It's not.'

'Don't give me this,' she said, and she stood on her tiptoes and poked him in the chest. 'You go and see her and you treat her gently. And know that you'll answer to me if you don't. And, no, there's no baklava for you until you make things right with Holly. She's borrowed swim clothes—that you have such a collection here for women to wear makes her more angry, by the way. As it makes me angry. You'll need to tread on eggshells to make your peace with that one.'

He walked across the island to find her. He could have taken one of the Jeeps but he needed time to collect himself. To figure out how to approach what came next.

It seemed that ever since the reporter had come to him with the news about Holly, he'd been moving on autopilot. He'd been trying to get answers fast, but now it behoved him to move a little more cautiously. Sophia was right. Nothing would be gained by having Holly as hysterical as when he'd last seen her.

Mind, it was hard for him to stay calm. The words of the reporter still bit deep.

'Did you know there's a child's grave on her property? The gravestone says "Adam Andreas Cavanagh. Died 7th October 2000 aged seven weeks and two days. Cherished infant son of Holly. A tiny angel, loved with all my heart."'

Adam Andreas Cavanagh. The name—what the reporter was suggesting—had generated a pain he'd never thought he was capable of feeling. Even before he'd worked back through the dates, he'd known the truth. For he remembered her saying:

'Your home's Adamas? I love that. Adam's such a strong name. If I ever have a son I'd love him to be called Adam.'

They'd been lying in thick grass on a rocky verge that looked out over her home. Normally the outback cattle station was dry and dusty, but the rains had come just before he'd left. The change to Munwannay had been almost miraculous, dust turning to verdant green almost overnight.

So they'd made love that last time on a bed of soft grass and wildflowers. She'd clung to him with fierce passion, she'd talked of naming a son—hypothetically, he'd thought—and then he'd left to get on with his real life.

Leaving behind… Adam Andreas Cavanagh. He had no doubt that the reporter's suspicions were right. Holly had been a virgin when he'd met her. It had to be…

But if it was, it was a disaster.

'I must have left an impression, then,' he'd joked to the reporter. 'For Holly to give her son one of my names. Maybe she hasn't met many royal princes. You'd think the baby's father might have been a bit resentful.'

It had been a remark meant to avert suspicion, but he wasn't sure whether the reporter had swallowed it. With the current scandals rocking the royal family, anything more could cause descent into chaos. The press knew it and was actively looking for trouble.

Holly was trouble. Holly screaming her head off because he'd had her brought here. Did she realize she might have the power to bring down the throne?

He walked round the final sand-hill before the beach Sophia had said she was on, and he stopped dead.

She was lying not ten yards away. She was wearing the bottom of a tiny, crimson bikini. Nothing else. She was lying face down but she was propped up on her elbows, reading, and he could see the generous curve of her lovely breasts. Her fair curls were tangled down her shoulders. She'd been swimming and her hair was still damp. She looked…free, he thought suddenly; free in a way he could never be. And quite extraordinarily beautiful.

The knot of anger and tension that had been clenched inside him for weeks dissolved, just like that. It was replaced by a sensation so strong he had to fight to stand in the one spot. She hadn't noticed his approach. He could just walk forward and lie down beside her, let his body touch hers, take her in his arms as he'd taken her all those years ago.

Right. He was here to avert calamitous gossip—not make more.

'Get yourself decent,' he growled in a voice he scarcely recognized, and her head jerked up and she hauled herself upright in fright, reaching for her discarded bikini top. She clutched it, hauling it against her but not before he'd seen what lay beneath.

She was almost ten years older than last time he'd seen her. She had a woman's body now. A full, sensuous collection of curves that together could make a man…

'What are you doing here?' she snapped, cutting across his thoughts. She frantically retied her top, then reached down and grabbed her towel, wrapping it round herself tightly and hanging on to it for dear life.

'I own the island,' he said mildly and waited for her reaction.

It didn't come. She didn't say anything.

'I need to speak to you,' he said at last. 'That's why I brought you here.'

'You could have telephoned. We aren't exactly in the Dark Ages.'

'No,' he agreed. 'But telephones are bugged.'

'Yours?'

'Yours.'

She gasped at that, incredulous. 'Why would anyone bug my telephone?'

'Because my entire kingdom wants to know what happened with us.' He hesitated. 'Let's go back to the house.'

'If you want to drag me back screaming.'

'Holly, cooperate.'

'Give me one good reason why I should.'

'You owe me the truth!' It was said with such passion that it brought her up short. Her eyes widened and there was suddenly a trace of uncertainty in her eyes.

'I owe you nothing,' she whispered.

'You bore my son.'

It was said with such heaviness, such dull certainty that it hurt. He saw her flinch. The fingers that had been clutching her towel so tightly loosened. It was as if she suddenly had nothing more to protect.

'I did,' she whispered. Her gaze met his, steady, unapologetic, but behind the defiance he saw a hurt that ran bone deep.

'You never told me.' The roughness had gone from his voice. The confused fury that had driven him for the last weeks had unexpectedly weakened.

'No.' It was a flat negative, nothing more.

He said nothing. There was almost perfect stillness around them—the faint lapping of the water on the golden sand but nothing, nothing, nothing.

Nothing to distract them from this thing that was between them. This awful, immutable truth.

'I believe I had the right to know,' he said at last, heavily, and he watched as the anger flashed back into her eyes.

'As I had the right to receive the letters you told me you'd write. Not a phone call, Andreas. Nothing. One polite note to my parents thanking them for their hospitality, written on royal letterhead—typed by some palace secretary—and that was it.'

'You know I couldn't…'

'Extend the relationship? Of course I did. You were engaged before you came to Australia. But we were kids. I was a teenager, Andreas. I'd never had a boyfriend. You had no right to take advantage…'

'It wasn't all one way!'

'It wasn't, was it?' she said, and he thought he saw a faint trace of a smile behind her eyes. 'But I was still a kid.'

That was the problem. He knew it. They both knew it. She'd been seventeen when he first met her. Seventeen. Not eighteen.

It made all the difference in the world.

'Did you know you were pregnant when I left?' he asked, trying to focus on the personal, rather than the political, ramifications of what had happened.

'Yes,' she said, and he flinched. Suddenly the personal was all that mattered.

'So that last time…'

'Oh, I didn't know for sure,' she said. 'My home is hardly the place where you can pop down to the supermarket for a pregnancy test. But I guessed.'

'Then why…'

'Because you were engaged to be married,' she said, sounding out each syllable as if she were talking to a simpleton. 'Andreas, I don't want to talk about this. Tell me, what would you have done if you'd discovered I was pregnant?'

'Married you.'

It was said with such certainty that she blinked. But then she smiled drearily and shook her head.

'No. That's air-dreaming. We talked about it—don't you remember? How we loved each other and wanted to be together for always. How you'd take me to Aristo and I'd be a princess. How my parents would cope without me and your father would forgive you eventually. Only there was already a princess, Andreas. Christina was waiting in the wings, and your marriage was meant to help to strengthen international ties. You talked about defying your father but you never once said you could break your engagement to Christina.'

'We were promised as children,' he said and he knew it sounded weak. It had sounded weak then, too. Holly hadn't understood how such marriages worked. How Christina, five years older than he, had been raised from childhood to see herself as his wife. Christina would never have looked at another man. To tell Christina—aged twenty-five—that he no longer intended to marry her, would have been personally devastating to her, as well as politically disastrous.

He had a duty and he'd known it. Holly had known it, too.

She shivered and her towel dropped. She bent to retrieve it but he was before her, wrapping it round her shoulders, ignoring her involuntary protest.

'I'm getting sunburned,' she said, flinching at the feel of his hands on his shoulders, stepping away from him, her voice flat and dull. 'I need to go back to the house. If that's all you want to say to me…well, you've said it. Can you arrange transport back to Australia immediately?'

'I can't do that.'

'Why not?' She hauled away from him, turning toward the path. *She was turning her back on him?* She shouldn't do that, he thought. To turn your back on royalty…

He could have her put in prison for insubordination.

But she was already walking away. He watched her and thought she looked tired. She shouldn't be tired. She'd had time here to rest.

There was a long, ragged scar running from the back of her knee almost to her ankle. It showed white against her tan. That hadn't been there before.

She was a different woman from the girl he'd fallen in love

with. But the girl he'd fallen in love with would never have been afraid of accusations of insubordination. Some things hadn't changed.

She wasn't waiting for him. She was simply ignoring him, trudging slowly back to the pavilion. He caught up with her in a few long strides and fell in beside her.

'What happened to your leg?'

'I don't have to—'

'Tell me? No, you don't. But I'd like to know. It's a nasty scar and I hate to think that you've been hurt.'

She cast him a look that was almost fearful. 'You think a cut on the leg can hurt me? That's a minor cut, Andreas Karedes. You have no idea what can really hurt. And don't you turn on the royal charm to me,' she snapped. 'I'm impervious.'

'Are you?' He smiled and she gasped and turned deliberately to face ahead.

'Leave me alone. You seduced me once. If you think you're seducing me again…'

'I just asked what happened to your leg. It's hardly a come-on.'

'I cut it on some fencing wire.'

'You were fencing?'

'Yes, if you must know.'

'Your father would never have allowed you to fence.'

'While you were around, no,' she said. 'There was a lot that didn't happen when you were around.'

'I don't understand.'

She turned on him then, her colour high. 'We were broke,' she said, through teeth that were suddenly chattering. 'I didn't know. No one knew. Our neighbours, our friends. No one. He hid it, my father. Our homestead was grand and imposing, and the landholding vast. You know my mother was minor European royalty? She never lost her love of luxury, and my father indulged her. They both assumed things would come right. They didn't, but that didn't stop them spending. My father borrowed and he borrowed and he borrowed.'

'He was rich,' Andreas said, stunned.

'He wasn't,' she snapped. 'So when I turned seventeen they hatched some crazy plan to have me marry wealth. My mother used her connections. She wrote to every royal house in Europe; every billionaire she'd ever heard of, offering a home-stay for young men before they took over their duties. You were the first who came.'

'There was money...'

'It was a façade. You remember the balls, the picnics, the splendour... Until then I was a kid being home-schooled because we couldn't afford boarding school. I worked on the farm, but as soon as you arrived I was off duty. I was a young lady. I was free to spend every minute of every day with you if I wanted. And of course it went to my head. I was free for the first time in my life and my parents were pushing me into your arms for all they were worth. Only then I got pregnant and you left and the whole pack of cards came tumbling down. My father was left with a mountain of debt. My mother simply walked out, and there I was. Pregnant. Desperate. And even lovesick, if you must know.'

'Lovesick,' he said faintly, but she responded with a look of scorn.

'Leave it. You want to hear the story? I'm telling you.' Her words were almost tumbling out, as if she was trying hard to get this over as fast as possible. 'So, pregnant or not, I had to work, and yes I have scars but the outward ones are the least of it. No, I didn't tell you I was pregnant even when my parents... Well, there was no way I was letting them coerce you into marriage. So I had my baby and I loved him so much he changed my world.' She faltered but then forced herself to continue.

'But...but when he was almost two months old he got meningitis and he died. That's it. End of story.' She closed her eyes for a fraction of a second and then opened them again. Story almost over. The hard part done. 'So there it is. I got myself a university degree by correspondence so I could teach.

I taught School of the Air like I'd always intended and that's the only money that's been coming into the farm for years. My father was incapacitated with depression but he wouldn't hear of selling the farm and I couldn't leave him. Six months ago he died. I put the place on the market, but it's too run down. It hasn't sold and I was planning to walk away when your thugs arrived. So what are you planning to do with me now, Andreas? Punish me more? Believe me, I've been punished enough. My Adam died.'

Her voice choked on a sob of pure fury, directed at him, directed at the death of her baby, directed at the whole world. She wiped her face desperately with the back of her hand.

He moved towards her but she backed away. 'No!'

'You called him Adam,' he said, hating to hurt her more, but knowing he might never get answers at any other time than now. Now when her defences were smashed. When she was so far out of control…

'Adam Andreas,' she whispered. 'For his father. He even looked like you. You should have seen… I so wanted you to see…' She gasped and it was too much.

He moved then, like a big cat, lunging forward to grasp her shoulders. She wrenched back but he hauled her in against him and held, whether she wished it or not.

He simply held.

She was rigid in his grasp, but he could feel her shoulders heaving. 'No…no.'

'Let it go, Holly,' he said, and held her tighter still and let his face rest on her lovely curls.

For a moment he thought she wouldn't let herself succumb to his attempts at comfort. The stiffness in her body felt even more pronounced.

And then, so suddenly he almost let her go, he felt the tension release. She let her body slump against him. He tugged her into him. Her face buried into his shoulder and he felt her weep.

It lasted thirty seconds at the most. He held her close, the most primeval of emotions coursing through his veins, all to do with protection, desire, possession, and then he felt her stiffen and pull away. This woman would not give in to tears easily, he thought as she hauled herself back from him and swiped her face angrily on her towel. He remembered her refusal to weep when he'd left. He'd seen the glimmer of tears and had watched her simply shut them down, hold them back.

She did so now. Her eyes, when she finally raised them to meet his, were cold and defiant.

'You have no right to make me feel like this,' she whispered. 'You have no rights at all.'

'I had the right to know my son.'

The words shocked them both. They were said with such a harshness that both of them knew it for an inviolate truth. She stared at him for a long moment, and then simply turned her back on him. Again.

'I know you did,' she said, starting to trudge again toward the pavilion. 'If he'd lived I'd have told you. I should have told you straight away. But I didn't attempt to hide him. If you'd contacted me… But of course you didn't. And you need to un-derstand. The moment you left my world fell apart. The social-izing we'd done had pushed us over the limit. The debt collectors pulled the place apart. They even took Merryweather.' Her voice broke and she paused, trying to regroup. She kicked the sand out before her in anger and she trudged on.

Merryweather.

'Your horse,' he said, stunned, thinking back to the beauti-ful mare she'd loved almost as an extension of herself.

'She was the least of it,' she said, hauling herself back under control with an obvious effort. 'She was a fantastic stock-horse and she was in foal to a brilliant sire. She and her foal were worth far too much to keep. My mother walked out, and my father went on a drinking binge that lasted for years. I kept my pregnancy from my father until I was six months gone, and by then you were married. By then my father knew that no amount of child support would save the farm, and I saw no point in destroying your marriage. I told my parents if they tried to black-mail you then I'd deny the baby was yours. I... I was just so tied up with putting one foot after another that I had no time to think of you.

'Or not very much,' she admitted. 'I had to keep the cattle alive. I had to keep my father from self-destruction. And maybe there was also depression at play as well. I told myself I'd write to you after the birth, but I was barely over the birth when... when...'

She stopped walking but she didn't turn. She took a deep breath, forcing the words out as if they still had the capacity to cut her to the heart. 'When Adam died,' she said, squaring her shoulders, every inch of her rigid with tension.

Andreas tried to imagine what that must have been like for her. He'd never had anything to do with babies. He thought of her holding a tiny child—the wild girl he'd fallen in love with, suddenly transformed into a woman. Holly breastfeeding. Holly sleeping with a baby beside her. Suddenly it was there, a mental image so strong it was as if he'd been there. Holly as a mother. The mother of his son.

'I don't know this...meningitis.'

'Lucky you,' she said drearily. 'It happened so fast... He woke in the night with a fever. I rang the flying doctor service at six a.m. They arrived at eight and he died on the plane to the city. They said it was so appalling a case that it wouldn't have mattered if we'd lived right by the hospital—there was simply no time for the antibiotics to work.'

'Was your mother...?'

'Nowhere. Back in Europe. If I wouldn't acknowledge you as Adam's father she washed her hands of me.'

'But your father took care of you?' The thought of her facing her baby's death alone seemed insupportable.

'Are you kidding? He'd gone on a bender the day my mother walked out and was still drunk. God knows where he was the day I buried my baby but he wasn't with me.' She shook her head. 'Leave it. I'm on my own. I buried my little boy myself and I've taken care of myself since. Now is that all? I don't know why you've brought me here, Andreas, but you might as well let me go. There's nothing left between us but a dead baby, and that's the truth. Let me go and be done with me.'

CHAPTER THREE

THEY walked back to the pavilion side by side. Holly said nothing and Andreas could think of nothing to say. He could barely remember the echoes of his fury that she'd borne his son and not told him. Her story had been flat and truthful and dreadful.

Her loneliness appalled him.

That he'd left her to face childbirth and the babe's subsequent death alone seemed unthinkable. He'd been so young. He'd left her to come home to a magnificent royal wedding. Thinking of Holly had hurt so he'd tried not to think of her at all.

He'd been a boy.

That was no excuse. He should have...

'There's no reason to berate yourself for what happened ten years ago,' Holly said with sudden asperity. 'Adam's death wasn't your fault. For the rest... I knew I was being seduced by a prince and I liked it.'

'You weren't...'

'Seduced?' she demanded with a trace of the old Holly. 'What do you call what happened between us? Hair like gold filigree, I believe you told me. Eyes like stars. Breasts like—'

'There's no need to—'

'There's not, is there?' she agreed and fell silent again.

'It was good,' he said cautiously, glancing at her sideways. Maybe he did remember the overblown compliments. Maybe he even remembered his older brothers coaching him.

'Being a prince has definite advantages where women are concerned.' He remembered Alex telling him this. 'There's hardly a woman you can't get into your bed. It's just a matter of a few pretty words and they're yours for the taking.'

It had been heady stuff for a young prince to hear. Heady advice for a young prince to live by.

Maybe, God help him, he'd even believed it.

'It was fun,' Holly conceded, interjecting over his thoughts. 'But before you get all smug, if I hadn't wanted to be seduced you wouldn't have had a chance.'

'As you don't want to be seduced now?' Hell, where had that come from? But the words were out before he could stop himself saying them.

Maybe it wasn't the wisest come-on. And it certainly wasn't the way to lead into Sebastian's plan for them.

She gasped. She stopped walking—and then she started again, very fast.

'We were children, Andreas. We're not children now. If you think you have a snowball's chance in a bushfire…'

He grinned, distracted as he'd been distracted years ago by her Aussie expressions. Flat out like a lizard drinking. Barmy as a bandicoot. Mad as a cut snake.

'I remember the way you talk,' he said and she glared back at him as if he were crazy.

'Shut up,' she snapped. 'Just shut up. If I get one more compliment from you I'll choke. How soon can I get off this place?'

'There are things we need to sort.'

'What things?'

'We do need to talk,' he said gravely, but she was hardly listening. She'd crested the last hill before the pavilion and was speeding up.

'So we speak at dinner?' he asked.

'Go home, Andreas,' she snapped.

'This is my home.'

'You live on Aristo. With your wife. With your children.'

'There is no wife,' he said. 'No children, either.'

She whirled to face him then, her face blanching. 'Oh, Andreas…' She swallowed. 'Not…not dead?'

'Not dead,' he said, fast, wanting desperately to take away the pain he saw surge behind her eyes. Of course. This woman had seen tragedy. It was natural she'd expect it in his. 'Christina and I never had children,' he said gently. 'We divorced six months ago.'

'Oh,' she said, her face still white. The pain in her eyes was replaced by blank acceptance. She turned away again. 'I'm sorry.'

But not very, he thought. Not even very interested. For a moment he came close to wishing that Christina had died, so the sympathy in her face would have stayed. What he saw now was something close to contempt.

It was a new sensation for Andreas. Women didn't show contempt to the royal princes of Karedes.

Women?

Yes, there had been women. Christina had been a faithless wife, finally leaving him for a shipping tycoon. And Andreas… well, the last few years hadn't been without their comforts.

They were being dredged up now, one after another, he thought bleakly, as the press scrambled to make the royal princes look a bunch of pleasure-seeking womanizers. Culminating in this. An accusation that had the capacity to bring down a throne.

The urgency of the current situation slammed back. Holly was assuming he could put her on a plane and send her calmly back to where she'd come from.

Maybe he could. If she could swear…

'Holly, is there anyone who could prove the baby… Adam…' he corrected himself hastily as he saw her face. 'Is there any way it can be proved that Adam was mine?'

Until now he'd thought she was so angry she could scarcely be angrier.

He was wrong.

She'd dropped her towel at some point and had simply left

it. She stood now, facing him, bare of everything but her skimpy bikini. She was only five feet four or so, but she looked much taller. She was all heaving bosom and flashing eyes—and temper to the point of explosion.

'I beg your pardon?' she said at last, dripping ice with every word.

But it had to be asked.

'I have to know,' he said. He was feeling sick at what he'd just learned but this couldn't be the end of it. What was at stake was too important.

'You want to know if I can prove you were Adam's father?' she demanded, incredulous.

'I know I fathered your child,' he said flatly. 'I accept your word, the dates fit and I know you were a virgin.'

'Thank you so much,' she said, scorn dripping as well as ice. 'But…'

'But what?' They were too close. She was glaring up at him, tugged so close he could feel her breasts beneath the fine linen of his shirt. Her anger was a palpable force, holding them together with fire.

'Holly, I'm in trouble,' he said simply. 'We're all in trouble. If anyone else can prove the baby was mine, then I'm going to have to marry you.'

As a conversation stopper it was magnificent. It set up a boundary over which Holly would not step. She stared at him for one long, incredulous moment and then she closed her eyes.

'You're mad and I'll have nothing to do with you,' she spat, and that was all she'd say. She wrenched herself away with a viciousness he could scarcely credit for a woman so small. She slapped his hands away and, unless he was prepared to hold her back with force, he had no option but to let her go.

She marched back to the pavilion with her head held high. Sophia met them at the main entrance as if she'd been on the lookout for them, her shrewd eyes filled with unasked questions.

'His Highness has had too much sun,' Holly said to her. 'I think he needs a doctor. I'm going to take a shower and cool off.'

She marched across the tiled courtyard to the apartment Sophia had obviously allocated her. She hauled the oak doors wide, marched in and slammed the doors so hard behind her that the ceiling fans in the vast entrance hall wobbled on their bearings.

Sophia and Andreas were left staring after her. And staring at each other.

'Do you want dinner?' Sophia said at last, though Andreas knew there were a dozen other questions her eyes were asking.

'In an hour.'

'I'd imagine Holly will have it in her room,' she said cautiously, staring at the very shut doors.

Enough. He was a prince of the blood. He was here with a mission. 'Holly will have her dinner out by the pool with me,' he snapped, a score or more of his exceedingly autocratic ancestors snapping to attention behind him, stiffening his spine. 'Tell her that.'

'You might want to tell her yourself,' Sophia said, still cautious.

'It's your place to tell her.'

'My Andreas is being a coward?' Sophia said and she smiled.

'Yes, he is,' he admitted, raking his hair and giving her a rueful smile. Autocratic ancestors might come at will, but they never hung round long enough to be really useful. 'Please, Sophia, would you tell her?'

'I'll tell her,' Sophia said and smiled up at him some more, and then reached up and raked his black curls back into place as she'd done when he was six years old. 'I'll tell her you're distressed and need to talk.'

'No…'

'You are distressed. You tell that one the truth,' Sophia said sternly. 'I've seen her long enough now to know that nothing but the truth will serve.'

He swam.

It was an hour until dinner, there was nothing to do but pace

and he'd wear a hole in the magnificent tiles in his bedcham-
ber if he paced as he felt like doing. So he abandoned himself
to the pleasure of his internal lagoon. The pool was a perfect
circle, with an island in the centre, set up with lounges, um-
brellas, a bar with every drink a man—or woman—would
want.

He wanted none of them now. He simply swam, circling the
pool over and over, his long, lean body cutting through the
water with the ease and grace that had come from years of hard
physical training.

Swimming was to Andreas a time of something akin to
meditation. A time when he could block out everything: the
demands of royalty; the problems with a disastrous marriage;
even the impending crisis of the missing diamond.

But he couldn't block out Holly. Not here. Not now. She was
in his thoughts every moment as he circled the pool, and no
matter how fast he swam there was no escape.

He'd thought he'd forgotten her. Ten years ago he'd walked
away from her because there was no choice. Now...now it
seemed there was a choice again.

He had to be disinterested. He had to explain things calmly,
setting the future before her in terms she must understand.

But she had a choice. He couldn't marry her out of hand.
Could he?

No, he conceded as he swam. The days of dragging an unwilling bride to the altar were long gone, and shame could no
longer be used as an incentive.

She'd been shamed before, when he'd left. The thought of
what she'd faced alone...

It couldn't matter. He had to put the gut-wrenching emotion
he'd felt as she'd described her baby's death aside. For now, for
his country's sake, he needed to be level-headed, sharp and per-
suasive.

But he didn't know how to be, when the moment he looked
at her he felt like a kid again; a young prince with the world at
his feet. With Holly at his feet...

Holly.

He had to get his mind clear. He had to get his arguments in order.

All he could think of was how beautiful she was. And that she'd borne his son.

He'd had a son and he'd never known him. The thought was enough to shift his foundations. To make him unsure of who he was in the world.

He'd let this woman down. She had to agree to his proposal. Somehow he had to make amends, but that had to fit with Sebastian's demands.

The demands of his king.

He'd know she could see him.

Every apartment in the pavilion looked over the pool. Andreas swam with the ease of a shark circling his prey, she thought uneasily, watching him rounding the island with lazy ease and a speed that looked deceptively easy to obtain.

Holly conceded that he looked magnificent, but then she'd thought he was magnificent once before. This time she had to use her head. This time she had to keep her emotions firmly in the background as she held Andreas at arm's length.

Or further.

He had to marry her? The concept was ridiculous. He was a royal prince. She was broke, a single mother of a dead baby. Her home was half a world away from here. Further.

Enough. She whirled away from the window, refusing to look at him any longer. His easy good looks, his wicked smile, his domineering personality…they had the power to rip her world apart as it had been ripped apart ten years ago.

She was not the same innocent as she was then. She'd been little more than a child. She was all woman now, and she'd meet him on her terms.

At dinner?

That was what he'd ordered and what he ordered was what Andreas generally got.

Not now. She had to stand up to him.

On equal terms, she thought, feeling desperate. She was still in her bikini. She had no clothes of her own here, apart from one battered pair of jeans and a tattered shirt.

She wouldn't see him like that.

Well, then.

She eyed the massive wardrobe with caution. Maybe Andreas had provided her with the weapons she needed.

It would take courage, but then…what did she have to lose?

Sophia provided a dinner fit for royalty—when had she not?—but this night the meal was enough to make even Andreas's eyes widen. He'd showered and dressed in casual trousers and an open-necked linen shirt, and then he'd thought better of it and donned a tie and jacket. It behoved him to step carefully, he thought. There were major decisions to be made tonight.

Sebastian's words were still ringing harsh in his ears. 'You'll have to marry her. There's no choice. If the child really was yours then a Cinderella wedding is the best we can ask for—a fairy tale to distract from reality. That's what the PR people are telling us. It'll take the sordid mess of your divorce away from people's minds. You'll be forgiven if you do the honourable thing, and there's very little honour in our family right now.'

So he emerged formally attired, he glanced at the amazing table setting—glimmering crystal and silverware, a table groaning with seafood, set up under a netted canopy under the stars—and all that was missing was Holly.

All that was missing was his bride.

'I've let her know dinner's served,' Sophia said, watching him cautiously from the shadows. 'But she says she's eating in her room. She's strong willed.'

'So am I,' Andreas growled, and strode along the courtyard to knock at her door.

No answer.

'Holly?'

'Go away.'

'Sophia will not serve you in your apartment.'

'Then I'll go hungry because I'm not eating with you.'

'That's childish.'

'So I'm childish. You, on the other hand, are overbearing, arrogant and crazy. Go away, Andreas.'

'I order you to—'

'Order away, you big oaf. I'm staying here.'

His face darkened. He stared at the door in gathering anger. Then he put his shoulder against the wood and pushed.

Nothing.

Damn, this was how they did it in the movies. He tried again, shoving with all his strength.

Nothing.

He'd get Nikos. But one last shove… He gathered himself, bunching his muscles in sheer frustration and shoved for all he was worth.

The door swung inward, unlatched, free, and he sprawled full length onto the bedroom carpet.

He lay, winded. Above him Holly stood looking down, seemingly solicitous.

'Oh, dear,' she said, her lips twitching. 'Did the prince fall over?'

He stared up at her and amazingly the corners of her mouth were curved into the delicious smile he'd fallen in love with ten years back. 'Do you need a hand up?'

He put out a hand without thinking. She tugged, he came up too fast and all of a sudden they were way too close. She staggered backwards, his hands came out to steady her and they were closer still.

She felt…fabulous. She felt like the Holly he'd remembered for all these years. The smell of her was reminiscent of citrus lemon; very faint. He'd always assumed it was her perfume but she'd hardly been given time to pack perfume.

And what was she wearing?

This was no cringing kidnap victim. Nor was it a woman

dressed to calmly eat in her bedroom. She was wearing a dress that was beautiful enough to make his eyes water. It was a simple jade cocktail dress, sleek, closely fitting, its tiny shoe-string straps holding it just barely above the lovely curve of her breasts. The soft silk clung to every gorgeous curve. A slit in the side revealed a flash of thigh so tantalizing that he felt his body respond in primeval need.

His hands tightened on hers involuntarily in a gesture of pure possession. He'd wanted this woman the first time he'd seen her, and he wanted her now.

But she didn't want him. Her hands came up, they wedged against his chest and she shoved so hard that he let her go. Why had he done that? It felt like tearing part of himself away.

She looked... She looked...

'You're staring,' she said, almost kindly. 'Don't.'

'Why are you wearing that?'

'What does it look like on me?' she asked, seemingly determined to be casual, even though he could see she was fighting the mounting colour on her cheeks. She deliberately twirled so he could see it from all angles—or maybe so she had some breathing space where she wasn't forced to meet his gaze head on. 'Compared to every other woman who's worn it?' she demanded, cutting across his thoughts. The amusement had gone from her voice and anger had returned. 'Dresses in every size, Andreas. Negligees, nightwear, even lingerie. How many women do you drag here against their will and then dress in your fancy outfits? This is some harem.'

'It's not a harem.'

'Not?'

Well, maybe. He thought back a few months to when Christina had finally achieved her precious divorce. 'You're free, brother,' Alex had told him. 'You set that island up for seduction and you're set for life. Fill it with things women love. Clothes that are worth a fortune. Seriously sexy stuff. The one thing you don't have on that island is shopping, and you need to make up for it if you want hot women. I'll tell you what—

as a gift to celebrate your divorce to that harpy I'll equip the wardrobes for you.'

He had. Six months ago Andreas had inspected the mass of clothes Alex—or, he suspected, one of Alex's mistresses—had chosen for his imagined stream of women and he'd laughed. Maybe it'd even be fun to use them, he'd thought.

But it hadn't worked out like that. Life outside marriage to Christina was infinitely easier, but seduction for seduction's sake didn't hold any appeal for Andreas.

Though seduction with Holly… He looked at her now, in her gorgeous dress, her eyes bright with anger, mocking him in a manner no woman had ever used in his presence…and he thought seduction was a definite possibility.

Not. He had a mission here. Fix it, Sebastian had said, and ravishing Holly against her will would fix nothing.

And, he suspected, his hand involuntarily fingering his cheek, it might even be dangerous. This woman had claws and she knew how to use them.

This woman was seriously sexy.

'So you're coming to dinner,' he said, for want of anything better to say. When what he really wanted to say was, Let's go to bed. Right here. Right now.

Thinking on, he didn't want to say anything at all.

But Holly had herself under control, and was calmly accepting his dinner invitation. 'If I must.'

'You must.'

'Fine,' she said flatly and walked out the door before he could respond.

He was left to follow and to think about where he could take this from here.

CHAPTER FOUR

THEY ate in pregnant silence.

Andreas was accustomed to silence. He and Christina had barely been on speaking terms for years, but palace protocol decreed they eat together so silence had been the norm.

But this was a different silence. It was a silence charged with a tension that was palpable, with anger and with…desire?

Yes, desire, Andreas thought as the meal wore on. For he couldn't keep his eyes from her.

She ate well; not selectively as Christina had done, but as if she was determined to enjoy every mouthful of the magnificent meal Sophia had put before them. Sophia beamed her pleasure as she served them, deeply appreciative of a woman who enjoyed her food. With Christina, Sophia had been absurdly formal, a servant who knew her place. Now, when Holly cracked a lobster claw too hard and the pincher sailed across the tiles, Sophia retrieved it and chuckled and Holly chuckled with her.

'You need to fight harder,' Sophia said, and was it Andreas's imagination or did she cast a warning glance across at him? Holly smiled at her, a woman to woman smile of understanding. They were friends, he thought. In the few days Holly had been here, Holly and Sophia had forged an unlikely friendship.

And there it was again, that stab of desire going deep into his gut. He loved Holly's smile. He loved that Sophia liked her.

Sophia was her friend.

Could he be her friend? No, he thought, revolted. He wanted far more from this woman than friendship.

Marriage.

Yes, but a formal marriage. Nothing more. For Sebastian's words had been unequivocal.

'The people need to know you've done the right thing, Andreas. But the marriage won't be long term. You marry her—give the country the fairy-tale wedding. That'll get us over our present crisis. You'll be seen as being honourable—as soon as you found out about the baby you did what was expected. Afterwards, we can say she's homesick for her country. She can return home quietly with the vague impression you'll visit in between royal duties. The thing will die a natural death. Problem solved.'

But what had seemed logical back in Sebastian's study seemed impossible here.

Maybe it had been a mistake to come here. How was he to propose a marriage of convenience when he knew she'd respond with anger? And what he really wanted… Well, that was impossible, too. There was no way he could ravish Holly against her will. He'd have Sophia after him with the branding iron. And to have her agree… The way she was reacting to him, pigs might fly.

Finally the meal was over. Sophia filled their wine glasses—though Holly had hardly touched her wine—and left them to it.

The night was truly lovely. There were fireflies flitting low over the pool, their tiny lights reflecting magically in the water's smooth surface. Sophia had thrown open the gates at either end of the pavilion and the soft sea breeze filtered through. The sky above them had a million stars, a vast continuation of the fireflies' reflection in the pool.

It was the most romantic of settings. It was a night for seduction.

'So now you've got me here,' Holly said, breaking into the silence, 'what do you intend to do with me?'

'I beg your pardon?'

'You wanted to know about Adam.' Her voice faltered as she said her son's name, but she forced it to steady. 'I could have told you what you needed to know of Adam in one phone call. Instead you commit a crime which could have you thrown in jail—any international court would agree. Prince or no prince, this isn't the Dark Ages. You've dragged me here against my will and you're in uncharted territory. You let me go now and I'll go screaming to the press.'

'You won't do that.'

'Tell me why I won't.'

'Your reputation…'

'My reputation?' She raised her brow in polite incredulity. 'What, I'll be revealed as a single mother? Shock, horror. You think I've hidden Adam's existence? Everyone at home knows I had a baby. I conceived Adam in love, Andreas, whether you knew it or not, and I've never been ashamed of it. If you or any of your people had approached me I would have told you about him, openly and honestly. He was the most perfect little boy and that we created him…'

She fell silent for a little, but then looked over the table at him, defiant again. 'So you're telling me the press could crucify me if they learned of Adam's existence? Not me. You maybe, Andreas, but not me.'

He nodded, rueful. 'Okay. Yes. They'd crucify my family.'

She raised her brow again in mock astonishment. 'You have to be kidding. Royals have been having babies on the wrong side of the blanket for generations. As far as I can see, there's even pride in it.'

'There's no pride in me for Adam's existence.'

'Then more fool you,' she snapped. 'You didn't contact me. You missed out on seeing your son. You missed his life, Andreas, and it's such a loss I can't even begin to make you understand.'

He couldn't think like that. It hurt, he discovered. He'd known of Adam's existence for less than a month but the knowledge had changed something inside that was fundamen-

tal. He wasn't sure how to deal with it. He didn't know if he
could. He just had to concentrate on the here and now while
he tried.

'Holly, I need to get to the point,' he said, taking a long swig
of his wine. Dutch courage? Maybe. 'Adam did exist. Someone
saw the gravestone. I gather you've had international buyers on
the place?'

'I have,' she said, sounding wary.

'Your land agent knew I stayed there years ago,' he said.
'He's touting that as a sales pitch—buy the place that once
hosted royalty.'

'I never said…' she began, revolted.

'Realtors will use whatever means they can to get a sale.' He
had to get this said. He had to block out the personal. 'So you had
a party of Arabian businessmen go through the place last month.
One of them saw the gravestone, saw the name and the dates,
wondered about the connection to me and mentioned it to his
cousin. Who's a journalist in Calista. So we have questions being
asked. And now you're saying it can be proved the baby is mine.'

She gasped.

'No,' he said, quickly, as he saw indignation flood into her
face again. 'I'm not questioning you, Holly. I accept that Adam
was my son.' Hell, that hurt to say. My son. For a man to say
such a thing about a child he'd never known… But he had to
continue, even if it meant being brutal. 'I mean outsiders,' he
said. 'If Adam can be proved to the world to be mine there's a
real chance his birth could bring down our throne.'

He had her attention then. He saw the change on her face.
Indignation and anger gave way to confusion. 'How…?'

'You were seventeen when he was conceived,' he said
wearily. 'It makes all the difference in the world.'

'How?'

'The age of consent here is eighteen,' he said. 'The king…
my father…was a known profligate. There was corruption and
scandal in the last days of his reign and there's been a massive
backlash.'

'So what's that got to do with me?' She sounded breathless, still confused.

'My family's enemies would go to vast lengths to bring us down,' Andreas said.

'Your father's enemies?'

'Let me explain,' he said, and then tried to figure out how to do so. It seemed so wrong. The only light was the candles on the table and the stars and the fireflies. They could hear the faint whoosh, whoosh of the surf from the beach outside. This setting was one of romance, seduction and passion, and yet he had to speak cold, hard, facts.

'You know the kingdom of Adamas is divided into two islands—Calista and Aristo,' he said at last. 'The Stefani diamond—a priceless stone of incomparable beauty—has always been central to our hold on the throne. The coronation charter says: No person shall rule Adamas without the blessing of the Stefani jewel.

'When the kingdom was divided into the two islands, the Stefani diamond was split as well,' he said, refusing to deviate from an explanation that he must make crystal clear to Holly. Everything depended on it. 'There's the royal family of Aristo—myself and my siblings—and the royal family of Calista. Each family has half of the Stefani diamond.'

'So?'

'So on my father's death we discovered our half of the diamond is nothing more than a paste copy. My father's marriage…well, to say the least it was dysfunctional. There were other women. Intrigue. Financial wheeling dealing. Somewhere along the line the diamond's been disposed of, and for us it means ruin.'

'I see.' But then she shook her head, her blonde curls flicking sensuously over her bare shoulders. 'No. I don't see.'

'We're at the mercy of the people,' he said. 'Or worse. Whoever holds both diamonds will rule both the islands, so if the diamond is found by King Zakari Al'Farisi of Calista then he'll hold all power. If, though, as appears to be the case, my father gambled the diamond or gave it as a trinket to one of his mistresses then power reverts to the people and public opinion holds sway. Rumours of my father's womanizing have been legion. My brothers and I have maybe…in the past…not been perfect. My brother Alex has recently married but that's not enough to stop indignation and a call for new rule. And the fresh news that I fathered a child when you were seventeen… My brother believes it's enough to topple us. Zakari may end up ruling us all.'

'That's some problem.' She lifted her wine glass and stared into its depths. 'But not my problem, Andreas,' she whispered. 'You walked away from me and didn't look back.'

'I never meant to hurt you.'

'No,' she said. 'I don't imagine you did. Nor did my parents. They threw us together hoping for a forced marriage or at least a fortune. And you… You didn't lie to me. I knew from the start you were promised to Christina. So did my parents, come to that—they just never imagined your sense of duty would override your decency.'

'My decency…'

'Yes, your decency,' she snapped. 'Your moral obligation to a girl who fell in love with you. You might still have been young, Andreas, but you were experienced. I, on the other hand, had no defences at all.'

'So…'

'So nothing,' she said wearily. 'Whatever moral outrage we might have created all those years ago, it's nothing to do with me any more. Give me a piece of paper to sign that says I release you from all obligations and be done with it. I'll sign. I just want to go home.'

'To a bleak bedsit while you teach kids thousands of miles away from you?'

'You've really done your homework,' she answered.

'I have, and you can't go home. The only thing that would save me—us—is a declaration that Adam wasn't my child. And you can't give me that.'

'No,' she said softly. She was looking directly at him now, meeting his gaze calmly over the table. She'd done a huge amount of growing up in the years since he'd seen her, he thought. The eyes that gazed at him were those of a woman: thoughtful, intelligent, even compassionate.

'I wouldn't ask…'

'You wouldn't ask me to make such a declaration?' She gave a hollow laugh. 'Says he who organized an international kidnapping. Well, maybe you will and maybe you won't, but it's not so simple. My mother holds copies of the results of Adam's DNA.'

'Your mother…'

'There you are,' she said, closing her eyes as if something hurt. 'I'm not completely without family. There's still my mother. When you left and everything fell apart she walked out. But she came back when the baby was born. For, of course, she knew who the father was. In the few days after Adam's birth I was ill—out of it. She told the doctors I'd need DNA samples to prove Adam's paternity and she took a copy of the results. But I guessed what she intended and was able to stop it.'

'Stop what?'

'Blackmail,' she said flatly. 'You were newly married. My mother saw Adam's birth as a great opportunity to make serious money.'

Hell. Maybe he would have paid, too, he thought, thinking back to Christina as a new bride. She'd been jealous right from the start. News of Holly's baby would have blown them apart.

'It's okay,' Holly said wearily. 'Or it was okay. My mother had just met another man. He had serious money and was giving her a good time. But there were things in her past I knew that…' She shook her head. 'No. It doesn't matter. But it meant that if she exposed you I could expose her right back. She knew her relationship would crumble if I talked, so she had a choice—shut up and enjoy her new lifestyle or take a chance on blackmailing you. She chose to stay.'

'Whew,' he said.

'Yeah, whew,' she agreed grimly. 'But if your reporters are fishing round now…my mother's situation has changed. She'll remember that piece of paper. Would the reporters pay?'

Would they ever? And if King Zakari found out… Yes, money would be offered. Serious money.

'She'll tell,' Holly said bleakly. 'I'm sorry, Andreas, but I can't help you.'

'Then it comes to this,' he said heavily, thinking his options through and accepting the course of action Sebastian proposed was the only one that could possibly work. 'We brazen it out. We say, yes, we were kids. We tell the public I didn't know about the baby but now I do I'll make reparation. We'll stand in front of my people with our heads high, Holly. But it's as I suggested on the beach. We'll stand together as man and wife.'

CHAPTER FIVE

SILENCE. Silence, silence and more silence.

Maybe he should have gone down on bended knee, Andreas thought as the silence stretched out. Maybe he should have handed over a diamond almost as big as the missing Stefani stone.

Or maybe not. He watched a host of emotions sweeping over Holly's face and he thought no, he had to play this straight. And he had to stay up his end of the table. For there was anger—unmistakable wrath. He didn't want to risk another slap.

'This is a real proposal,' he said as the silence stretched out and the tension became almost unbearable. 'I'd marry you in all honour.'

'Thank you,' she said. The words had been meant to come out as bitter sarcasm, he thought, but they broke mid try and ended up almost a frightened squeak.

'It's the only solution.'

'For who? There's two people in this equation.'

'I could settle your father's debts. I know you're feeling honour bound to meet them. I could remove that pressure and more.'

That was enough to take her breath away. She pushed herself back in her chair and gazed at him as if he'd produced a hand gun. 'How do you know?'

'I know all about you,' he said, forcing his voice to be gentle in the face of what seemed almost to be terror. 'From the time we had the whisper about the baby my brother's had investigators working round the clock.'

'Your brother.'

'Sebastian. Heir to the throne of Aristo. If this blows up then he loses the throne.'

'You all lose the throne,' she whispered.

'My siblings and I are mere princes and princesses.'

'Mere,' she said, mocking now. She pushed herself to her feet. 'Don't do this, Andreas. You can't buy me.'

'I knew ten years ago that I couldn't buy you,' he said ruefully. 'Do you remember I asked you to continue to be my mistress?'

'And do you remember my answer? I would have thought you could still feel it.'

'I do,' he said ruefully and touched his ear—an ear that many years ago had been soundly boxed. 'But this isn't then, Holly, and it's not an affair I'm asking. I'm offering marriage.'

'And I'm supposed to be flattered. You haul me here—'

'Why don't we forget about the kidnapping?'

'Why don't we?' she jeered. 'Four thugs drag me forcibly from my home and dump me here and then you calmly propose marriage… Yeah, forget the first bit, think, Ooh, the great Prince Andreas of Karedes has asked me to marry him, swoon, swoon, of course, Your Majesty, how could you ever think I could refuse?'

'You don't think that maybe you're getting carried away here,' he asked dryly. 'It wouldn't be *that* bad.'

'Christina got out of the marriage pretty fast. How many women did you have on the side while you were married to her?'

'These things are understood—'

'In royal marriages,' she snapped. 'Not the marriages I know.'

'What marriages? The one-sided affair your parents had? And you… How much experience have you had? And you're hardly likely to marry for love now.'

Uh oh.

She'd moved behind her chair and was holding onto it as

if she needed its support. Her knuckles were so stretched he could see the white of the bone under her taut skin. Maybe he'd gone too far…

'So I'm an old maid as well as everything else,' she hissed. 'A fallen woman; a spinster past my use-by date. Expected to fall on my knees in gratitude at your very generous offer.'

'Look,' he said, trying hard to figure how to placate her. She was breathing too fast. Her breasts were heaving with indignation and her face was flushed with fury. How to really mess up a proposal… He had to get this back on track. 'Holly, we really need it.'

'You know, I can't figure out even that,' she said. 'You took me to bed when I was seventeen and that can't be changed by anything we do now.'

'No, but I can be seen as honourable,' he told her. 'If it's only a matter of time before reporters talk to your mother then it has to be a fait accompli. When the first accusation comes I need to be able to say yes, it's a shock that I fathered a son. I can't understand why Holly didn't tell me. We were romantic kids. However now I've found out, of course I'll do the honourable thing. Luckily I'm single again, so I can give her my hand in marriage.'

'She doesn't want it,' she snapped.

'Why not?' It was a harsh, loaded question and it brought the silence back. She stared across the table at him as if he were an alien—as if she'd never seen him before in her life.

'Because I'm free,' she managed at last and it was such an unexpected response that it was his turn to stare.

'Pardon?'

She closed her eyes. 'Okay, Andreas. I'm trying to get my head round this. You need to do the honourable thing. Marry me. But that means I'd be in the royal fishbowl.'

'I don't understand.'

'You know, when you used to tell me about your life back here, the money you had at your disposal, every indulgence, parties, women, luxury beyond belief, I wasn't even jealous.

You know what I thought? I thought poor little rich boy. Maybe that was even why I fell into bed with you. I felt sorry for you.'

'Sorry,' he said, astounded.

'I've seen what can happen to royalty,' she said. 'It gives me the horrors. I want to walk down the street and buy a can of baked beans and a packet of Tim Tams for dinner, any time I want.'

'Baked beans?' The conversation had suddenly headed at a tangent he couldn't follow. Candlelight. Fireflies. A soft warm wind. A wedding proposal. And the talk had turned to baked beans.

'What would happen if you want baked beans for dinner?' she demanded.

'I wouldn't,' he said, revolted.

'We're playing make-believe here. Indulge me.'

'I'd ask Sophia…'

'Right. You'd order baked beans from your domestic staff. And Sophia would raise her eyebrows and say "What does Prince Andreas want with baked beans?" But of course your wish is her command so she'd write the royal shopping list and servants would go to one of those shops with the fancy insignia saying Suppliers to Royalty. And the shop assistants would have a chat about why you want baked beans and what are Tim Tams anyway, and when they find out then they'd say why doesn't Prince Andreas buy local food. Maybe Aristo produces excellent chocolate cookies, so why aren't you supporting local industry? Maybe it'd even make the papers.'

'You've thought this all through,' he said, puzzled. 'You've thought about your life as a royal bride. Does that mean you've thought of marrying me before?'

She stared across the table at him and her expression changed. The anger was replaced with confusion.

'How dare you?' she whispered at last.

'You have thought of marrying me?'

'I carried your child for nine months. Of course I thought of marrying you. What woman wouldn't? It was a fantasy solution to my problems. But it was only ever a fantasy and I got over it.'

'So how long did you carry me in your heart?'

Her jaw dropped. 'What?'

'My investigators tell me there's been no man for years.'

Her breath sucked in with fury. 'Your investigators can go to hell.'

'The locals say Adam's death shattered you. Was part of that me? That I wasn't there?'

'Leave it,' she whispered, but she might as well have yelled. She stood, holding onto the table with fingers that were clenched so hard her knuckles still showed white. 'Of all the arrogant, conceited—'

'We were in love.' He rose, watching her steadily across the table. 'We were in love, Holly.'

'You don't know what love is. You who never wrote…' Her voice broke. 'I hated you. I just hated…' She gasped and pulled back from the table.

It was too much. He moved involuntarily, striding the few steps to her side before he realized he'd intended it, grasping her hands, holding her against him. She fought, wrenching away, but he held her regardless, holding her tight until he felt the fight go out of her. He felt her slump against him, defeated by the strength of her emotions.

The present disappeared. Suddenly nothing else mattered but that this was Holly. And he'd distressed her.

What was he doing, proposing marriage when the past was still between them? When he'd caused her so much pain.

He touched her hair with his lips, smelling the clean, citrussy fragrance of her. Feeling her palpable anguish.

'Holly, I wish I'd known,' he said softly into her hair. 'I'm so sorry you were alone. And I so wish I'd known about Adam.'

'He was…he was…'

'I can imagine.'

'You can't,' she said dully, the anger seemingly spent as anguish took over. 'He was your son and you never knew him.'

He didn't release her completely, but let her stand far enough apart so he could look down into her face.

'I am sorry,' he said again, for it was the only thing he could think of to say. It wasn't enough. He knew it the moment the words were out of his mouth.

'Why didn't you write?' she demanded.

'I was marrying another woman,' he said. 'I was promised in marriage. That didn't mean I didn't think of you every day for years.'

'Says you,' she answered and he shook his head.

'You must believe me, Holly.'

'I must believe you so I'll agree to do what you want now?'

'Holly, this marriage…our need to make this right…it isn't just for me and for my family.'

'Isn't it?' Her voice was pure scorn. 'I'd imagine King Zakari would make a very good king for both islands. The islands would be joined as one kingdom again. I expect you and your family would keep your fabulous wealth. So what's the problem?'

'Half our island could lose their livelihood,' he said flatly, holding her wrists tighter still. 'My father has tied the money in the island so close to our own fortune that if we're no longer here then half the industry on Aristo will fail. I agree,' he said as she opened her mouth to retort. 'It's a dreadful situation and given time we will be able to fix it. But time's not on our side. We have to have a coronation and soon. If we can't find the diamond then the people get to choose who rules them. Like you, they'll say we wish to stay to feather our own nest. But it's not true, Holly. We need to stay to keep the island financially stable.'

'And you expect me to believe that so much that I'll marry you.'

'Many women…' he said softly, changing his grip so she received the utmost semblance of tenderness he could manage. The utmost entreaty. 'Many women would give their eye teeth to be a princess.'

'Are you crazy?' She wrenched backwards, so abruptly that he finally let her go. 'Andreas, I know nothing of your world. How can you ask it of me?'

'Find out. Come back with me to the mainland. Meet my family.'

'And be photographed from every angle as the woman you seduced years ago? To have a whole country saying I should marry you? No, thank you.'

'Then decide now,' he said. 'Marry me now and go back to the mainland as my bride. But you must marry me.'

'I must do nothing. There's nothing in it for me.'

'How can you say that?' He didn't have a clue where to take this from here. His instinct was to shut up, to leave it, but the need was too urgent to let it go. 'There's a crown. There's money.'

'I've done very well for all my life with no crown and no money.'

'Then what about me?' Andreas said, watching her face. Knowing there were more than cold hard facts ruling her. 'I ask again, have you done very well without me?'

'I've had to,' she managed through clenched teeth. 'Do you think I haven't tried to forget?'

'But yet you've remembered,' he said softly, and he moved again. But slowly, giving her time to back away if she wanted. Purposefully. 'As I've remembered.' He reached for her hands again and held, but lightly, no pressure. But he pulled her in all the same, the force not of physical strength but almost as a magnetic pull so two bodies that belonged together came together.

He'd been wanting to do this for so long, since the first time he'd seen her, angry and miserable and frightened on the plane. Maybe since he'd left her all those years ago. When she was little more than a girl.

She was no girl now. Nor was she frightened. Despite Alex's outrageous wardrobe collection with its heavy sexual connotations, Holly's no would mean no.

But she was still furious, and she was still confused. He could feel it in the rigid way she held her body, yet she still allowed herself to be tugged against him. It was almost as if she needed to see if there was something there.

There certainly was. On his part at least. He felt his body respond as her beautiful curves came in to lightly brush against him, and it was as if he were touched by fire.

Her dress was truly lovely and had been worn by no woman until tonight. It could fit no other, Andreas thought as his hands slipped to her sides and felt the way the silk clung to every inch of her as if it were another skin.

He could feel the warmth of her body under the silk. Involuntarily his hold tightened. His hands found the small of her back and pressed her tight against him. There was a moment's resistance but then she yielded, letting her breasts be crushed against his.

Holly.

He'd forgotten a woman could be so beautiful.

'Do you remember the first night I kissed you?' he whispered and she gave a sharp shake of the head.

'Liar,' he said, smiling softly. He remembered it like yesterday. His green girl. It had been the first night of his arrival. Her parents had given a ball in his honour. She'd been dressed all in white. When all the guests had gone he'd been left in the homestead's massive ballroom and she'd been sent in to help clear glasses. She'd dropped one. It had snapped in two, they'd bent together to retrieve the broken portions and had almost hit heads. But then…they'd been so close…to kiss her had seemed the most natural thing in the world.

As it was now. His long, tanned fingers tilted her chin so his mouth could lower to meet hers. Wondrously she didn't resist. For whatever reason, the fight, the anger had faded. He felt her hands on his hips, and gloriously they were tugging him closer.

And then the sensation ceased as his mouth met hers.

The years slipped away. Right there. Right then.

He'd thought his memories of what he'd had with Holly all those years ago had been tinged rose-coloured with distance and regret. When he'd made love with his wife he'd thought longingly of what he'd felt with Holly. It had distressed him unutterably. Finally he'd dismissed the memories as a boy's romantic imagining, unfair to Christina, to be blocked out as fanciful and unreal.

Only it wasn't. He knew it now, the moment he touched her.

For this was no kiss. It was the searing fusion of two bodies kept apart for too long, two bodies meant to be together as one.

Forged by fire... That was how it felt. The heat was not imagined—it was real—a flame consuming all, making his hold on her tighten so he was crushing her against him as his mouth devoured hers, taking as well as giving, demanding her response, needing her as he needed a part of himself.

Holly. His heart, his home. The words slashed into his consciousness. How could he have forgotten his desire for this woman? He'd pushed it into the dark recesses of his memory, yet here she was, exquisite, desirable—and free.

He was free as well. Fix it, Sebastian had ordered, and he could, simply by taking this woman as his wife.

Holly. His captive wife. He was tasting her, loving her, wanting her. She was all his, folded into him, with his body moulding against hers. His hands slipped to her hips, cupping the smooth rise of her thighs. He was tugging her closer, closer, but still she wasn't close enough. Without breaking the kiss he lifted her, up into his arms, against his heart.

For one glorious moment he felt her submit. He felt her arms come round his neck, deepening the kiss, clinging, merging into him. She was his. His!

But then... He shifted slightly, to gain a better hold, and the movement broke the contact. Just a touch—a heartbeat. But it was enough. He felt her hands come between their breasts and she was pushing away.

No! He tugged her close, intensifying the kiss, but she was hauling away, breaking the contact.

'Andreas, stop.'

And he knew what she was saying. For already he was turning towards the bedroom, intent, desperate, wanting only to be as close to this woman as he could possibly get.

He could take her. This was his woman.

But this was Holly, and somewhere beneath the smouldering desire of a royal prince was a boy who'd been in love. Instinctively, involuntarily, he hesitated and looked down at the woman in his arms. Her eyes were dark with passion but there was something else. He expected anger but the anger was gone. In its place…

Trouble. Doubt.

'*Agapi mou…*' he said softly. 'My heart, what is it?'

'I don't want this.'

'You don't want me?'

'That's not what I said,' she whispered. 'I think I want you as much as life itself—I always have—but, Andreas, you have to give me time to think.' It seemed as much as she could do to get the words out.

'If you think then you'll refuse me,' he said simply.

'Then maybe I have to refuse you,' she managed. 'Please, Andreas, put me down.'

'And if I don't?' He didn't want to release her. Damn his scruples. He was prince here after all, and this was his woman. This was how he felt about her. She was the mother of his child and he wanted her so much his thighs burned.

'If you're the man I think you are then you won't take me against my will,' she whispered and it was said with such assurance that he groaned inwardly. But he set her to her feet. It felt like cutting his heart out. To lose her…

'You want me as much as I want you,' he growled. 'Admit it.'

'My body wants you,' she said, and suddenly her voice was even; sure. 'But my head's saying we're crazy. My head's saying we ended up pregnant before when precautions didn't work. Will I risk ending up with another baby—maybe even another loss and grief—because of one night's passion?'

Her words were enough to sober him. It was enough to look into her eyes and see the truth written there—a pain he hadn't shared, which had torn her in two.

So he released her. She staggered as he set her away from him, and it was as much as he could do not to react, to watch her gravely as conflicting emotions flitted over her face, as she stepped away from him—as sense won over raw desire.

'I...need space,' she said unsteadily and backed toward her room.

'But you'll think of what I've said?'

'Yes, I'll think,' she whispered. 'And, Andreas?'

'Yes?'

'I'll think because you *did* set me down,' she said. 'I'll think because you showed honour. Despite all that's gone before, I trust you. If you say you need to marry me for your country's sake, then I believe you. But that doesn't mean I agree. I need to get it right in my own head first. You have to give me time.'

'I—'

'Don't say any more. I can't afford to listen.'

'Holly—'

'No.' She blocked her ears and she tried for a smile—a smile of a child in mischief. It almost came off. With her ears firmly blocked she turned away from him. 'Lalalalalalalalala,' she sang at the top of her voice. 'Lalalalalalala.'

And, still singing, she fled.

He turned and Sophia was watching. She was holding a tray as if she was about to clear things from the table, but he knew she'd been standing there, listening.

'Were you about to hit me with a wine bottle?' he asked ruefully, and she smiled at him, but her smile held sympathy.

'I know you, my Andreas. You would not hurt her more.'

'I would never hurt her.'

'You already did.'

'Did she tell you that?'

'Rumours,' she said simply. 'They've reached even here. I heard you fathered a child with this woman?'

'And...'

'And this one has lost a baby. I know this. I talked to her about my sons and I saw her pain. And now you stand back with honour. So what will you do?'

He stared down at her, his old nurse, a lady in her sixties, bossy, matriarchal. His servant.

His brothers might raise their brows in supercilious disdain and walk away. He could not.

'I don't know,' he admitted.

'You want her.'

'I'd forgotten how much.'

'Then you need to woo her,' Sophia said wisely. 'You have to be gentle. Give her time.'

'There is no time. I have to get this sorted.'

'You rush this and you'll end up with nothing.'

'She must—'

'There is no must about it. She's a smart lady and she will not take kindly to musts.' Her wise eyes creased into a smile. 'She will make you a woman in a million. You and Christina…no and no and no. But you and this Holly…'

'Sophia, leave it.'

'I leave it,' she said, and to his astonishment she reached up and kissed him, something she hadn't done for twenty years. 'I leave it to you. To your good sense. To your brains, hey, and not to your balls. That's what got you into this mess. You and your brothers and your father, messes all round. Now your brains have to get you out.'

She thumped him on the chest and chuckled, then carried her tray serenely out to the pool to clear the table.

Holly heard the gentle murmur of their voices. She couldn't hear individual words—just that Andreas was talking. It must be to Sophia.

She was leaning heavily against her closed and locked bedroom door. It seemed too thin. It was no protection.

Sophia would protect her.

Not against herself.

This was Andreas she was talking about. She'd dreamed about Andreas for years. He was here. He wanted her. All she had to do was fall into his arms and be his princess.

See, there was the rub. It scared her so much that it overrode even the way her body reacted to his. She'd heard him tell of his family: his brutal father, his aristocratic mother and sisters, his brothers—sexy, powerful men who took what they wanted and held.

She knew nothing of their world. To give in to Andreas's blackmailing—for that was what it was—was to abandon herself to his lifestyle; to give up all she'd ever known.

It was to abandon hope of going home. To Munwannay.

There was nothing there for her.

Her son's grave was there. It was home.

Her home could be here.

As Andreas's accessory? For that was what she'd be. She was fighting to get her breath back; fighting to make herself see sense. He'd made no declaration of love. He'd simply said he needed to marry her to get himself and his family out of a political mess. In return he'd pay for her father's debts. Great. That left her…where?

They should have talked tonight. It should have been a business discussion, she thought, pressing the back of her hand against lips that felt swollen, bruised, still hot from his touch. Maybe they could work something out.

But how could they work out anything when the way she felt about him got in the way? There he was, outside talking calmly to Sophia, and she was in here like a trembling virgin.

And likely to stay here. For there was no way she was opening the door, when the minute she saw him sense gave way to…

Lust.

It was as simple as that.

Or was it?

The voices faded. There was a clink of glasses—that'd be Sophia clearing the table. Andreas would have gone. Where? To bed? To calmly think of what other ways he could coerce her to marry him?

Marriage to Andreas…

The thought was like watching the sky open—there was no way she could see through to the other side and the thought of what lay beyond was so unimaginable that she couldn't do it. To hurl herself into the unknown… It seemed unthinkable.

But she had to think about it. She had to go to bed now and calmly consider whether such a marriage was possible. Andreas had said his country depended on their marriage. That was very well, but he was looking out for his country. He had his whole kingdom looking out for him—and she was alone.

She left the door and sidled to the drapes of the windows overlooking the pool. She slipped one back just a little so she could see.

Yes, Sophia was there, calmly gathering glasses. She looked up as the chink of light behind the curtains revealed she was being watched.

She straightened and met Holly's look full on. And then she smiled. And winked. And put down her tray of glasses, put both hands in the air and crossed her fingers.

Then she calmly went on gathering glasses.

Holly smiled.

No, she wasn't completely alone. She had one ally. Maybe…just maybe…

Just maybe one ally wasn't enough. She had to figure this out. She wasn't about to step into a royal goldfish bowl without knowing the facts.

They had to keep their hands off each other and they had to talk.

Talking was never going to work. How the hell could he talk her into something when he couldn't make sense to himself? He couldn't think past the fact that she was Holly and he wanted her so badly he was practically on fire.

He'd been raised to think marriage was a duty. Royal marriages were political gamesmanship. Passion was something you had on the side. His parents' marriage had been loveless. Even when he'd been with Holly all those years before, when they'd talked wildly about running away, the duty that had been instilled in him since birth took precedence.

But now…suddenly he was in a situation where he was being ordered to marry a woman who set him on fire.

Take it easy. Act with care. This was too precious to mess with.

But he couldn't take time. The hounds were baying. Sebastian would be here himself any minute to marry them by force if he didn't get this right, and he knew enough of his brother to believe that force was an option. Sebastian cared about his country in a way their father never had. He'd make a good king, and if all that stood between him and that kingdom was a slip of a girl…

Hell.

He walked out of the pavilion, down to the beach. He had so little time. Holly said she needed thinking space—she did. But he couldn't afford to sit back and wait for her to come to her verdict.

So what to do, short of firing Sophia, hammering down Holly's bedroom door and taking things to their natural conclusions. Which might not exactly work against Holly's spirited will. He'd known her as a girl, proud, independent, strong. She'd lost none of it; had gained more.

She was a woman in a million. He wanted her.

So tell her. Make love to her in the literal sense.

She'd believe him why? He'd been married to Christina. He hadn't been in contact with Holly for years. How could he persuade her how he felt, when he didn't know how he felt himself?

He did know how he felt. He stopped and stared out over the moonlit sea.

He wanted this woman. He wanted her more than life itself. If he had time he'd woo her as she ought to be wooed. He'd love her as she deserved to be loved.

So compress it. See what you can do in the time you have available. Think, man. He had to talk her into a short-term marriage at least. That'd buy him time.

He'd brought her here as his captive. What would keep her?

He forced himself to keep walking, thinking back to all the things he knew of the Holly he'd once loved. He conjured up her memory. Holly, wild and free. Holly, meeting him that first

morning when her father had brought him home, coming out
to the veranda, her old dog by her side.

He stopped.

It was a wild thought. Stupid. Sentimental. But this was no
ordinary need. What was needed was a gesture.

He was already turning back to the pavilion. He had work
to do this night. Thank God for the Internet. Thank God for
servants back on the mainland. He'd wake half the palace up
to get what he needed.

So little time…

He had to move.

CHAPTER SIX

IT WAS ten in the morning before Holly ventured to open her bedroom door. Sophia was sweeping the tiles around the pool—normally something Nikos did. Holly had been listening to her singing as she worked for the last hour and she'd finally figured Sophia was giving her reassurance that it was fine to come out. Not that she felt very reassured, but the moment she opened the door, she was.

'He's gone,' Sophia said and Holly gasped.

'G…gone.'

'He says he should be back tonight but he commands you not to worry.'

'Not to worry… What sort of a command is that?'

'He says go for a swim. Enjoy the day, hey? You are not to trouble your head. But first, breakfast.'

'I don't think I'm hungry.'

'Of course you're hungry,' Sophia said and beamed. 'Courtship always makes a girl hungry. When such a man looks at you with such eyes…ooh, all the senses come alive. Smell, feel, touch, taste… I've been young too, remember.'

'Courtship doesn't come into this,' Holly said, trying not to sound cross. She was wearing one of the most demure outfits from Andreas's outrageous wardrobe—a silk kimono. It covered her but not enough. Still, if he'd really gone… She peered around the courtyard as if she thought Sophia might be telling lies. As though Andreas might be yet to pounce.

'He's really gone,' Sophia said, smiling.

'Where?'

'Who knows? The royal princes...they are here, there, everywhere. The fuss about the old king's death is such that there are a million things to do. His mother may want him home.' Her face softened. 'She's had a hard time of it, the queen, no matter how brave a face she puts to the world.'

'I wouldn't know.'

'That's right. You've never met her. There's so much in front of you,' Sophia said and beamed.

Oh, goody. There was a reassurance.

'But you need feeding,' Sophia said, watching her face and deciding, obviously, that Holly needed distracting. 'You want to talk to me as I cook?'

'I can cook my own toast.'

'You're to be a princess,' Sophia said seriously. 'You need to get accustomed. You make your own toast—you offend a whole hierarchy of kitchen staff.'

'Really?'

'Really,' she said. 'Me, I don't mind for you are not yet a princess. But when you are...' She was still watching Holly's face, but it was as if this was too important not to be said, just because she was risking upsetting the girl in front of her. 'When you are, you'll be taking on a whole role. You represent our country. You are royalty.'

'I'm not royalty.'

'What I see in Prince Andreas's eyes...you will be.'

She wasn't royalty.

She ate breakfast—as much toast as she could get down without choking—and then she escaped to the beach. Sophia packed her lunch so she could stay as long as she wished. 'I'll send word if His Highness returns,' she told Holly and Holly thought it sounded like a warning.

But there was no escape. She was on Andreas's island. She

was bound to Andreas's rules. She was bound to wait for Andreas, and think and think and think.

He didn't come. She'd know if he came for if he'd left by plane he'd return by plane, but as the sun sank low in the sky she'd seen no sign of him.

Was it safe to go back to the house? It had to be. She was weary of lying on the sand trying to sort out her thoughts; floating in the surf trying to block out memories of last night's kiss; trying to read and seeing only Andreas instead of the print on the page.

Nothing was clear except her fear for the future and her longing for the past.

She walked slowly back to the pavilion. Sophia and Nikos were in the kitchen—she could hear them arguing as they commonly did when they were alone. Loud, voluble arguments, highly passionate over who knew what. They'd been married for forty years, Sophia had told her. Forty years and five children. What did they have to be passionate about?

Why was she feeling like this? So lonely she could weep. She'd been solitary all her life. For the last few years it had just been herself and her father and her job, and her students were dislocated voices on the end of the radio. Now she was with people, yet her sense of alienation was so strong it was threatening to overwhelm her.

Maybe it was seeing Sophia and Nikos and what a long-term marriage could be.

Maybe it was seeing Andreas again and seeing what could have been if they'd been different people, in different worlds.

Maybe she could marry him. Maybe it wouldn't be worse than living alone for the rest of her life. Maybe…

Maybe nothing. A plane was coming in fast from the east, a black blur against the sky. Andreas. She looked up and practically whimpered—and bolted for the safety of her bedroom.

'Dinner is served.'

The knock on the door wasn't Sophia's stern rap, or Andreas's autocratic thump. The voice was that of Nikos.

They'd sent a stooge, Holly thought. Nikos was timid around her. She couldn't yell at him.

Nor would she.

Dignity. There was the thing. She'd spent the last hour trying to summon it. She'd decided to wear the same dress as last night—the way Andreas's eyes had devoured her then, she wasn't giving him the satisfaction of having something new to look at.

Boring, boring, boring, she thought. He was a prince. He might well be accustomed to a new woman a night. If he was going to get bored with her, it was better that she knew it now.

Or whatever. Nothing she was thinking was making sense. This whole situation didn't make sense.

So go out and get it over with.

She opened the door. Nikos was waiting, smiling anxiously. He beckoned toward the dining table set once again under the stars.

Andreas was already seated, but he rose the minute he saw her. He was dressed to kill. Full evening attire. A dinner suit of deep, rich black, his white shirt brilliant against his dark skin. His eyes were black as night. He smiled at her and his smile flipped something inside her that stayed decidedly flipped.

He was sex on legs, she decided. It wasn't fair for a guy to have so much…so much…Andreas.

'You look beautiful,' he murmured, crossing to meet her, and she tried to glower.

'I look exactly the same as last night.'

'Not so. Your nose has started to peel. Just a little.'

'Leave my nose out of it.'

'But it's such a beautiful nose…

'Andreas…' Her voice broke and he stepped back. He'd been about to lightly touch her nose. Now he looked down at her in concern.

'You haven't had a good day?'

'What do you think?' she snapped. 'You give me these appalling options and then you walk away and leave me with nothing to do but think and think and think.'

'So what have you thought?' he asked gravely and she tried to make her mind focus.

What had she thought?

'That you're a nutcase,' she muttered. 'That what you're demanding is unbelievable. Totally unjustified.'

To her astonishment he smiled and kissed her lightly on the forehead, then led her over to the table.

'I agree. I thought so last night. I left you and thought what we were asking was a one-sided agreement where we win. You get to play a princess but I, of all people, should accept that this is no great bargain.'

She felt as if all the wind had been sucked out of her. Andreas held back the chair and waited 'til she sat. She plumped down and stared at him.

'Well, then?' she managed.

'Well, then,' he agreed gravely, and rounded the table to sit opposite.

'So I can go home?'

'You see, you can't,' he said apologetically. 'The fate of too many people would be changed irrevocably for the worse if you refuse to marry me.'

'Then nothing's changed.'

'Only my attitude,' he said softly. 'And the rules. I've spent the day negotiating. Oh, and shopping.'

'Shopping,' she said blankly. 'You're kidding.'

He smiled again. 'Sophia?' he called.

Nikos had disappeared back to the kitchen, back to Sophia's comfortable presence. But he came out now, holding the door wide so Sophia could come after him.

Sophia was carrying…

A puppy.

It wasn't just a puppy. Holly rose in astonishment as she saw the creature held in Sophia's ample arms. It was a border collie, a ten-to-twelve-week-old bundle of wriggling pup, black and white, with big, intelligent eyes and a tail that was threatening to wag so hard a lighter pup might have taken off like a hovercraft.

'He's attached to you already, Your Highness,' Sophia told Andreas, reproving. 'He didn't like you leaving him in the kitchen. See? He finds you and his tail starts to whir again.'

'What…?' Holly could barely get the words out.

'You see, there was something absent,' Andreas explained. He didn't walk forward to the pup but instead stood back and watched Holly's face. 'Yesterday I saw you and I thought there was something missing. And then…it came to me. From the first time I saw you back at Munwannay, you had a shadow. Always. A black and white shadow wherever you went. Deefer, I believed you called him.'

'Deefer Dog,' Holly murmured, stunned.

'An ancient cattle dog.'

'A border collie.' Like this pup. She couldn't keep her eyes off the pup in Sophia's arms.

'My people told me everything about your circumstances,' Andreas said, still watching her. 'But there was no mention of a dog. There was no dog on the place when our people inspected it.'

'I haven't had a dog since Deefer died.'

He frowned. 'Deefer was an old dog when I was there.'

'Yes,' she said, not trusting herself to go further. In truth Deefer had lived for only three weeks longer than Adam. Her baby and then her dog…

'Can I ask why you never bought another?'

'My father wouldn't have one.' The puppy was wriggling in excitement. She longed to reach out and touch him…

She wouldn't. This was seduction at its finest.

'But it's a farm. A working farm,' Andreas said, obviously still waiting for an explanation. She had to try and give him one.

'Yes, but…it was also my father's folly. Deefer wasn't Deefer's real name. He had a pedigree a mile long. All our dogs did. He was Cobalt Royal Rex or some nonsense. Deefer for short. But when he died that was it. My father had such pride— he'd never have a mongrel on our place and pedigree working dogs cost a fortune. I was never permitted to have another dog.'

'You were never permitted...' Andreas's face was calmly assessing. 'Yet according to my sources, you did all the work.'

'It was my father's farm. He made the business decisions.'

'He made the decision to run the place into the ground rather than sell up and move on while he could.'

'It was my decision, too,' she snapped. 'You think I didn't have a choice? But I loved it. I love it still. Adam's still there—and I want to go home.'

She gulped and dug her fingers into her palms and fought desperately for control while Andreas and Nikos and Sophia watched gravely on.

And then, as if coming to a decision right there, right then, Andreas lifted the little dog into his arms and he carried him across to Holly.

'Sit,' he ordered and she sat, for she couldn't think of anything else to do, at the elegant table with the exquisite silverware and crystal and candles.

He put the pup on her knee and he lifted her hands and placed them on the pup's collar.

'This is my troth,' he said gently.

'Your troth,' she said numbly.

'My vow,' he said, and then as Nikos and Sophia went to move away he made a curt hand signal for them to stay. 'No. I want witnesses. This is not for public consumption but I know that you two can be discreet. You two of all our people will know what is happening. Holly, I'm asking you to marry me, for the sake of our people. For the sake of our country. But I'm saying that I'll not hold you to this marriage for a moment longer than needs be. As soon as the fuss has died down—as soon as it's seen that I've done the honourable thing by you and that my family can't be called to account—we can't be dispossessed by our past—then you can go home. Back to Munwannay.'

'Back...'

'Yesterday I offered to pay your father's debts,' he said. 'But I watched you last night and I thought of what you faced alone and I thought it's not enough. So what I'm offering is your life back. I give you Deefer Two.' He smiled wryly at the pup. 'Or whatever you wish to call him. And I give you Munwannay. I've arranged for my people to buy it outright at the price you've been asking. The deeds will be given to you on the day of our marriage. Plus a marriage settlement that will be generous enough to enable you to farm the place with everything you need and more—for the next fifty years if you like. This will be yours, Holly. I can't take away my requirement that you marry me. You must. But this, I believe, is the honourable thing to do. All you need to do now is say you will and the thing is done.'

She gazed up at him, astounded beyond belief. Deefer Two wriggled in her arms and her fingers automatically started scratching behind his ears. He wriggled ecstatically, turned and gave her a long, slurping kiss from the chin to the forehead.

It had been years since she'd been kissed by a dog. And last night…she'd been kissed by a prince.

One thing at a time. Deeds to a farm. Marriage to a prince. Puppies were easier.

'How did you find…?'

'I worked,' he said, his eyes crinkling into laughter. 'All last night. I wanted a pure-bred collie dog that looked like Deefer. Right down to the white tip on the end of his tail. I put every available servant back at the palace onto it. From dawn I've had people ringing breeders across Europe.' He shook his head. 'You have no idea… I thought the Stefani diamond was price-less, but what we had to do to get you this pup…'

But he'd done it. Her prince. Her Andreas.

He was watching her closely, his dark eyes hooded, trying to conceal his emotions. But he was anxious. She could see a level of anxiety that couldn't be suppressed.

Did he think she was still going to refuse?

Maybe she should. But.

But this man could order a small army to search for a dog for her.

And more. This man had said she could bring his country

to ruin by refusing to marry him. He'd said his country's future depended on their marriage.

Against all sense, she believed him.

And if she believed him, was there a choice? What was she but a failed farmer, a teacher who could easily be replaced? She was nothing against the fate of a country.

In the scheme of things, what price marriage? If it meant she could go home again…

Could she?

Of course she could, she thought, trying to make her dizzy mind focus. What was she doing, dithering? The Royal House of Karedes was wealthy beyond belief—she'd always known that. What Andreas was offering was nothing in the light of his vast wealth.

And he meant it, she thought, dazed. This was no clandestine promise. He was making this offer not in private but in public, witnessed by Sophia and Nikos. It was a business proposition, no more, no less.

So…

So all she had to do was put aside the ignominious way she'd been bundled here against her will and take it from here.

And all she had to do was put away the way just looking at Andreas made her feel. As if there were something else possible behind a curt business arrangement. As if there were a love that had blazoned forth ten years ago and hadn't died.

Both things had to be ignored. Andreas was a prince of the blood. She knew that. She'd always known that. He took his pleasures where he willed. He'd just come from a marriage that Sophia had told her was tempestuous—a jealous hell from day one. He had a wardrobe full of exotic clothes on his exotic island, waiting for woman after woman after woman.

He wanted a new bride like a bad smell.

But this was a business proposition. She had to make herself see it as that. Business.

And in her arms… His troth.

The pup was a pretty funny troth, she thought, and she rose

to her feet and hugged the little dog close. His troth. Better than any diamond.

Deefer made it personal. Deefer made it seem…almost right. Almost as if there were some desire.

'You say…you're inferring we can divorce later on,' she said, trying to make herself think. 'But your divorce to Christine…'

'Was different. Christine used the occasion to bad-mouth me at a time she knew we were vulnerable. The timing was awful—scandal after scandal was rocking the palace. The lies she's told about me are one of the main reasons why it's imperative I'm seen as doing the right thing now. If you agree I'd ask that our marriage stay in place until Sebastian ascends to the throne. After that it doesn't matter what the people think of me. But Holly, I need this marriage. Our country needs this marriage. You have to believe me.'

'But if I believe you…there doesn't seem much choice,' she managed, and it was really hard to get even that much out. 'I'd have to marry you.'

'Is there anyone else?' he asked suddenly. 'I assumed…'

'Your people didn't find that out?'

'They said they thought not. Are they right?'

'Of course they're right,' she snapped before she could stop herself.

He smiled. 'That's a blessing.'

'For who?' she demanded.

'For me,' he said and had the temerity to grin.

'So you're free to marry him?' Sophia had been quiet long enough. She was practically jiggling with impatience. As they turned to look at her she gave a shamefaced smile. 'It's just… Your Highness, I have soufflés in the oven.'

'Then for the sake of the soufflés, Holly…' Andreas said, and his grin deepened.

And all at once Holly was smiling back, caught in the web of wonder she'd been trapped in ten years ago.

But… She couldn't be illogical. Even for the soufflés. She had to be…businesslike.

'So it's to be a temporary marriage.'

'Yes.'

'I can go home when I want?'

'As soon as the fuss dies down, yes.'

'You'll pay all my father's debts.'

'Of course.'

'You'll give me working capital as well?'

'Yes,' Andreas said. 'Anything else?'

'I can keep the pup?' Holly demanded, refusing to be distracted.

'He's yours. He'll need to be quarantined when he goes back to Australia, but I'll cover the costs in the marriage contracts.'

'So I'll have real, fully legal contracts.'

'If you want, then yes.'

She stared at him. He gazed calmly back, waiting for her decision. On the sidelines Sophia started jiggling again and looked despairingly toward the kitchen. She looked so desperate that Holly allowed herself to be distracted. The big picture was just too hard to focus on. So…why not focus on the detail?

Soufflés. Maybe soufflés were as good a reason as any to agree to a marriage she thought of as mad.

Was she mad? Probably, she thought. She felt as she had when, as a little girl, her father had taken her to a huge swimming pool in Perth. When he wasn't looking she'd climbed the diving tower, right to the top. Before she'd known it she'd been at the edge of the diving platform, and older, competent divers had been queuing up behind her waiting for her to dive.

'Are you going to dive or not?' a kid had asked scornfully and she'd looked down at the water way below her in horror—and she'd jumped.

And that was what she did now. Crazy or not, she believed what Andreas was telling her. And if she believed him…there didn't seem to be a choice.

'For the sake of the soufflé, then,' she said, forcing her voice to be calm, steady, all the things that she absolutely wasn't. 'For no other reason in the world, other than one small pup and a soufflé. Yes, Your Highness, I agree to marry you.'

What did she do after she'd just agreed to marry a prince? She ate soufflé, of course, a feather-light confection of cheeses that melted in her mouth and felt as insubstantial as the night.

Everything felt insubstantial. She felt as if she were floating in some weird bubble. Any minute it'd burst and she'd be catapulted back to her lonely life; the realities of coping with Munwannay by herself.

It'd happen. But it'd happen with enough money for her to make her property viable.

She was trying to stay distant from the man seated at the other side of the table. She'd agreed to marry him, but it was a bargain. A means to the end for both of them.

She'd need to buy in cattle, she thought. Good cattle, the kind she'd always dreamed she could run at stud. She could rebuild the garden. She could get the dry rot out of the floorboards. Maybe she could also think about doing what she'd always wanted—taking in select holidaymakers who wanted a real cattle experience in the outback.

It'd mean it wouldn't be so lonely.

She hadn't set Deefer down. The pup had had a very long day and was more than content to lie draped over her knee while she ate her soufflé and the rest of the magnificent dinner Sophia put before her.

And all the time Andreas watched her, his eyes dark and fathomless.

'This is what you want?' Andreas said at last as Sophia poured coffee and left them.

'Do I have a choice?' she asked, surprised.

'I can't coerce you,' he said. 'You know that. But I believe it's a fair bargain.'

'It is.' And of course she wanted it. Munwannay was where Adam lay. To be given the ability to stay there, for always…

'The divorce won't be possible until after my brother is crowned,' Andreas reminded her, and that hauled her thoughts away from one tiny grave and back to the man across the table from her. 'It seems presumptuous to talk about divorce before we're actually married,' he said. 'But I believe it's better that we have a plan.'

Plans sounded good. What was in her head now was an enormous knot of confusion. If he could somehow unravel it into bits she could understand then she might be able to cope.

'Tell me where we go from here,' she asked, and the little dog on her lap looked up at her as if in concern. She hugged him tight—a warm, familiar certainty in the face of internal chaos.

'We need a royal wedding,' he said. 'Not a huge affair—we'll leave the pomp and pageant for Sebastian, but the people will react well to a proper wedding.'

'I can hardly wear white,' she said and his brow snapped down.

'Of course you can wear white. It's not as if you've carried some other man's child.' It was said strongly, angrily—even possessively—and Holly flinched.

'No,' she murmured. 'Only yours.'

'So it means you can be a true bride if you wish,' he said. 'And maybe it'd be for the best if you are. There's rumours sweeping the country that I seduced you and I abandoned you. That your child died through poverty and neglect. I know,' he said as her eyes widened in shock. 'We'll set the story straight. But your isolation has meant that people will feel sorry for you, and maybe we have to play to that. The fact that you've had no other man—as far as we know—makes it possible for the people of my country to believe that you can be a truly worthy bride.'

'Oh, very good,' she managed. Only it wasn't. Here were the echoes of an anger that had been put aside for a little. 'So if I'd, say, had another boyfriend or six in the interim it would have been much…'

'Better,' he finished brusquely. 'If my people believed you were a trollop, then I might not have to marry you.'

'You don't have to marry me.'

'I do have to marry you,' he snapped. 'I have as little choice as you.'

Her coffee suddenly tasted like mud. She set the cup down on the delicately etched china saucer and pushed it away from her.

'So we have two people forced into a royal marriage of convenience.'

'That sums it up.' He sighed and looked across the table at her. 'Don't look like that. You were starting to look…better. More cheerful. Like there was an advantage to this somewhere.'

'There is,' she said and hugged her dog. 'Deefer and my farm. I'll need to figure the quarantine regulations for getting him back into Australia.'

'The breeder gave me the details but let's not apply for that just yet,' he said. 'Let's get married first.'

'So…when?'

'Three days.'

Her eyes flew to his, shocked. 'Three days?'

'Back on the mainland. I'll introduce you to my family and we wed that afternoon.'

'You must really be scared.'

'My brother thinks he's about to lose the crown,' Andreas said. 'Yes, he's scared. But so is half the country. We will not be swallowed by Calista.'

'And I'm the pawn…'

'We're both pawns.'

She ignored him. Or she was trying to ignore him.

'Why?' she said at last. 'Is there anything you're not telling me?'

He shook his head and she thought suddenly he looked dead tired. He'd been up all night trying to sort her a dog, a deal, a future? And flying back and forth collecting Deefer. She had a sudden urgent desire to go round the table and run her fingers through his dark hair. Hold his face against her breast as once she'd done, oh, so long ago.

It wouldn't work. They were adults now, with adult responsibilities. And surely she had an adult's mistrust of showing her heart on her sleeve.

'So…so how bad was your divorce?' she asked suddenly, seemingly out of nowhere, but in fact it was something she really wanted to know.

Sophia had told her the country was up in arms about Andreas's immoral behaviour, but she'd also said, 'But don't believe a word of it. Christina lied about Andreas from day one. She has powerful friends, that one, and she knows how to manipulate the press. Prince Andreas has been made to be the villain and he's too much of a gentleman to put them right.'

Holly looked across the table into Andreas's eyes and she saw the confirmation of what Sophia had told her. The country might be accusing the royal family of being immoral but she'd never believe it of Andreas. He might be a prince—he might be so far from her world that she could barely touch him—but she believed in his honour.

Today he'd worked on her behalf; he'd given her something he believed she truly wanted. So now…

She had a choice. She could go forth, kicking and screaming into the future, bewailing it wasn't right, it wasn't fair. Or she could start playing the part. She could even have…fun?

'I wouldn't mind being a bride,' she said cautiously, and she saw shock register.

'You wouldn't mind…'

She lifted an after-dinner mint from the middle of the table and bit into its creamy centre. There might well be advantages to royalty. One of them might be the seriously good chocolate. But… 'I won't wear a bustle,' she told him. 'No bows, either. But if there's a crown or a tiara or something, I don't mind a bit of bling.'

'Bling…'

'Diamonds are good,' she said, striving for insouciance.

'You can hardly wear the Aristo crown,' he said dryly. 'It might be gorgeous but there is the little fact that the diamond in the middle is paste.'

'Then I won't wear it,' she decreed. 'No paste for this princess. I want fabulous.'

'Fabulous.'

'Yes, fabulous. If we're stuck in a royal marriage, then why don't we give the whole country their money's worth?'

'You mean it?'

'I mean it.' She focused on her mint, trying to sound airy. 'I mean, if we both go into it pretending we hate the idea...what sort of impression does that give? That we're both wimps?'

'No one could ever say you're a wimp.'

'Nor you,' she said and eyed him with distinct approval. 'Not in that outfit. Golly, Andreas, who does your tailoring?'

'How would I know?' He rose and moved around the table so he was standing beside her, looking down at her with his hooded, enigmatic eyes.

'That's right,' she said, trying not to sound self-conscious. Trying not to sound as if he was standing too close and she was too aware of it. 'I forgot. You have a whole retinue of tailors.'

'Who'll move heaven and earth to sew you a wedding dress in time.'

'That'll be nice,' she said and smiled up at him and that was a mistake. Big mistake. For he was smiling back at her, with that devastating smile she'd fallen in love with ten years ago and had never fallen out of love with.

Deefer was on her knee. It was Deefer who saved her, for Andreas put his hands under her arms and would have tugged her up, only of course if he had then Deefer would have been caught under the table edge. The little dog forced Holly to plump back down again. She pushed the chair sideways and got to her feet herself, holding her dog like a shield.

'I need to go back to the mainland tonight,' Andreas said and she must have looked as she felt, for he took a step towards her. She took a very fast step back.

'I...why?'

'Because we're getting married in three days,' he said, as if that explained all.

'So you have to…what, send out invitations?' She was so far at sea she was drowning but she didn't know how to pull herself out.

'I guess I do,' he agreed, managing a smile, but his eyes didn't leave hers. There were messages zinging back and forth that she had no hope of interpreting.

'Is there anyone you'd like to invite?'

'How many people do I know here?'

'We could charter a jet from Australia. Do you want your mother to come?'

'She comes and the wedding's off,' she snapped before she could think about it, and he grimaced.

'Right. I remember your mother.'

'I try and forget her. We haven't spoken for years.'

He was still watching her with that rigid constraint. He was holding himself back, she thought, and she couldn't figure out why. And…holding himself back from what?

'Is there really no one you'd like to ask?'

'I'm on my own, Andreas. Apart from Deefer, that is.'

'When we're married you'll have the full royal family behind you.'

'Until I don't. This is a mock marriage,' she said sharply.

'No. It's a real marriage.'

'Until you figure out the politics. You don't want a wife, Andreas, and I want to be home.'

'I guess that's right.'

This formality was crazy. It was as if they were stepping on eggshells.

'So when will I see you again?'

'Georgiou will fetch you on the morning of the wedding. He'll take you straight to the palace. We'll be married in our private chapel, with just the people we absolutely have to have there.'

'Like your mother?'

'Like my mother, the queen. And my brother.'

'Who's going to be king.'

'That's right.'

'I think I feel sick,' she said. 'What on earth will they think of me?'

'They'll be grateful.'

'Yeah, right,' she said. 'Andreas, they're royal.'

'So am I, yet it didn't prevent us…'

He stopped. She stared up at him, trying to read what was going on behind that enigmatic expression. Nothing. Whatever he'd been about to say was to be left unsaid.

'I guess we're a man and a woman when it's all boiled down,' she whispered at last. 'I guess the fact that you're a prince is no big deal.'

'As you say.'

She summoned a smile. 'I don't have to promise to obey, do I?'

'I…no, if you don't want to.'

'You're going to make me sign a pre-nup?'

'I suspect…the lawyers will want…'

'I suspect the lawyers will want, too,' she said and then hesitated. 'Tell you what. Get me a lawyer, too.'

'Pardon?'

'It's all on your terms,' she said, trying to sound as if she knew what she was talking about. 'I mean, you've given me Deefer and you've given me promises but I just have your word.'

'You can take my word.' He sounded offended and she shrugged.

'Of course, but I'm a tadpole in an ocean here. You're talking contracts? So should I. I want an Australian lawyer to go over anything you want me to sign.'

'Where am I going to find an Australian lawyer?'

'I don't know. You found me a collie dog. You're good at finding stuff.'

'Holly…'

'You think I'm stretching the friendship?'

'I don't think you're stretching anything. But you can trust me.'

'Yes, but I'm still going to be on my own,' she said, deadly serious now. When she looked up into his eyes she forgot stuff—she didn't make sense even to herself. But it was true; she was a tadpole in the vast sea of royalty. This was her life. In a few weeks she'd be back in Australia and this would be a dream, and if Andreas's promises didn't come through…

'You can trust me,' he said again and she blinked and nodded.

'I know. But I still want my own lawyer.'

'Why?'

'Because I'm scared,' she snapped. 'Because I'm just me and I'm about to put on a wedding dress and marry a prince and I reckon even Cinderella shook in her glass slippers when it came down to it.'

He smiled then. The hooded restraint slipped a little. Then, before she could guess what he intended, he stepped forward and lifted Deefer from her arms.

He set the little dog carefully on the ground. 'Go sniff,' he told the pup. 'I have to talk to your mama for a minute.'

Then he straightened and took her hands in his.

It was such a fast, instinctive action that it was done before she could react. Before she could think about stepping back.

But she didn't step back. Somehow this moment was too big for scruples. She'd just agreed to marry this man. In three days she'd stand beside him and say I do. She could scarcely shrink from him.

And it wasn't as if she was scared of him. It was just…just…

'I will not let you be hurt by this,' Andreas said gently and her thoughts stopped operating as such. Something deep inside turned into this crazy sort of mush. She gazed up at him, saw his gentle smile and, yep, mush, mush, mush.

'Andreas…'

'I will keep my vow to you,' he said. 'Holly, I've hurt you enough. You marry me and I'll set you free. I swear.'

And then, before she could respond, before she could even think of responding, he lowered his mouth onto hers.

It was a kiss to seal a contract. No more. No less. But it was no light kiss. It was harsh, demanding, possessive. It set a seal on what had been said this night. The pup might be a token of softness, even affection, but this was a business deal with the fate of the country at stake. His kiss said as much. It seared into her, a welding together of two halves of a whole.

Gainsay me at your peril, the kiss said, and it was so different from the kisses they'd shared in the past that it might as well have been a different man. It was a different man. This was Prince Andreas of Karedes, protecting his country with a marriage of convenience. Taking her as his wife.

The kiss lingered until there were no doubts left.

Tonight he'd shown tenderness. He'd not lie to her. But she would be his bride.

And she wouldn't argue. Despite her fears, despite her qualms, she released herself in the kiss. She felt his hands grip her, tugging her hard against him, and she opened her lips and surrendered herself to him.

She might be his captive wife but she'd make no complaint. She'd struck her bargain. She'd go down this path as this man's bride.

And maybe…

'I have to go,' he said regretfully at last, and he put her away from him.

But still she thought.

Maybe, she thought, as he bade her a curt goodnight and left to organize the next part of his long night—the plane ride back to the mainland—just maybe the next few weeks might be a sight more exciting than the last ten years, stuck grieving on an outback cattle station.

Just maybe…

No. There was no maybe. This was a short business deal and then she'd be sent back to her life.

She'd go back to her life, she corrected herself as Andreas disappeared into the night and she turned to go back to her luxurious apartments. Alone.

For she did want to go back to Munwannay. Only…not just yet.

CHAPTER SEVEN

THREE days later.

It all seemed a bit rushed to Holly—a bit crazy—but the plan was that she leave the island for the mainland, she go straight to the palace and wed before the day was out.

She hadn't seen Andreas. There'd been one curt phone call. 'It's organized,' he had told her. 'Or it will be organized. There'll be a meeting with your lawyers and ours. You'll need to sign the contracts. Sophia has taken your measurements. All you need to do is come.'

'Um…my lawyers?'

'I've employed the best for you,' he said, and there was a tinge of grim humour in his voice. 'And, believe me, they're good. They're screwing us down on detail like you wouldn't believe.'

'I don't think I need…'

'You don't know what you need,' he told her curtly. 'Neither do I. We're doing what has to be done but I'm putting as many safeguards in place as I can think of. How's Deefer?'

'I…he's great.' Deefer was her one sure thing—a fluff ball, alert and intelligent and raring to bond with her. If she hadn't had Deefer she would have gone nuts. To sit on the beach and think of nothing but her impending wedding…

'Don't let that nose get any redder, will you, my love?' Andreas said softly, moving on. 'It'll clash with the pink roses my mother plans to decorate the chapel with.'

And he was gone, leaving her to wait. And wait and wait and wait. And go quietly nuts.

But the wedding day did happen. Sophia entered her room at dawn, pushed the drapes wide and beamed.

'Happy is the bride who the sun shines on.'

'You must have a whole country of happy brides,' Holly said, feeling really wobbly and sounding grumpy. 'This country's too sunny by half.'

'So smile,' Sophia said. 'Your wedding day…'

'It's not a true wedding.'

'Is it not?'

'You know it's not,' she said crossly. 'I'm his captive wife.'

'Ah, but his non-captive wife…' Sophia said softly. 'Christina…now there was a disaster. If that was the best the royal family could come up with then maybe his captive wife is who he should have had in the first place.' Her smile faded and she crossed to the bed and looked down at Holly—and at Deefer whose small black nose just happened to be sticking out from under the duvet. 'I'm thinking my Andreas found his bride ten years ago—he just never knew he had her.'

'Don't be ridiculous,' she whispered, feeling more terrified by the minute. 'You know this is just convenience. You know he doesn't want a bride.'

'I know you have a chance,' Sophia said and put her hand on Holly's cheek in a fleeting gesture of blessing. 'I know my Andreas has been raised as a prince, to know what is due to him. But I also know that he has a heart and that heart has needs. Don't you fail to take your chance for lack of courage. Now…' Her smile softened but Holly saw lists line up in triplicate. 'Shower. And then…I've laid out what you're to wear on the helicopter. You'll be photographed briefly in transit to the palace as you'll be photographed from every angle today.' She peered down at Holly's nose and she sighed. 'You're still peeling. What royal bride peels? Holly, Holly, Holly, what is Andreas to do with you?'

'Marry me?' Holly whispered in a tiny voice.

'Well, of course,' Sophia said as if that was a dumb response. 'But then what?'

And then the day started. It was okay back on the island—there were only Sophia and Nikos to see her off, Sophia sniffing into her handkerchief and Nikos just sniffing.

She sniffed herself. She sat in the back of the helicopter and hugged Deefer and decidedly sniffed. Georgiou was her pilot but she was damned if she was talking to him. She was dressed to kill in a slick little crimson suit with stiletto heels—Sophia had decreed nothing in the lavish wardrobe suitable for her first introduction to the country and had ordered Georgiou to bring this to her.

She looked as good as she could do—apart from one peeling nose.

She should have left Deefer behind. 'I'll mind him,' Sophia had promised. 'And Andreas can have him flown over after the wedding.' But he was coming with her. Her one true thing.

Not her husband?

Andreas was waiting for her. The royal family was waiting for her. The whole damned country was waiting for her.

She hugged Deefer and she stared out the window at Andreas's lovely island hideaway growing smaller and smaller in the distance.

And then she saw the mainland growing larger.

'Would you like a drink before you land? There's some in the cabinet by your side,' Georgiou said diffidently through the headset and she flashed him a look of hatred.

'I'd rather choke than accept a drink from you, you kidnapping toe rag.'

'I was only following orders.'

'Right. Well, my orders to you are to keep as far away from me as possible.'

'I believe I can't do that. I'm allocated as your personal bodyguard.'

'Oh, my God,' she said with loathing.

'So you'll just have to get used to me,' he said. 'Now, drink?'

'I'm tempted,' she muttered. 'Very tempted. Is Andreas meeting the plane?'

'He won't see you until the wedding,' Georgiou said, shocked. 'It's unlucky.'

'So he's not meeting the plane.'

'I believe the entire royal family is meeting the plane,' Georgiou said. 'Except Andreas.'

'Oh, goody,' she whispered. And reconsidered. 'Georgiou?'

'Yes, ma'am.'

'I will have a drink,' she said in a small voice. 'A very small one. But, Georgiou?'

'Yes?'

'Also a very strong one.'

They were there. Lined up like in a Christmas pageant. On the tarmac with a red carpet rolled out so their precious royal feet wouldn't have to touch anything so plebian as concrete.

She recognized them from photographs. Sebastian, Crown Prince, as handsome as his brother, looking stern, autocratic, determined. Queen Tia, elegant, composed, but with the trace of trouble behind her elderly eyes. And grief, Holly wondered. She smiled now for the cameras but her glance kept wandering to her eldest son. She'd gone through the death of her husband, the realization that he'd betrayed her, and that he'd sold or given away the diamond that held the country together. All these things Holly knew, but the face Tia presented for public consumption was almost serene. She'd been schooled for public life.

Who else? Alex, the prince who'd given Andreas his outrageous wardrobe, wouldn't be here. He was on his honeymoon, Sophia had told her. That was part of the problem for Andreas—with so much to do and the search for the diamond taking so much time the royals were overwhelmed by work.

Andreas's two sisters were there. The brat pack, Sophia

labelled them. Kitty and Lissa. 'They love nothing better than shocking the press,' Sophia had said, but these two beautiful women were watching Holly approach and Holly thought judging her seemed pretty high on their priority list right now.

'They're waiting for you,' Georgiou said.

'I want...Andreas.' She sounded like a pathetic child but she couldn't help it.

'He'll be waiting for you in the chapel.'

Right.

She gulped and held Deefer tighter. And walked forward to meet her future.

And after that the cameras took over. There were flashlights, flashlights and flashlights, so many that when she thought back to that day all she could remember was a blur of white light. There was a brief hiatus when she was ushered into the presence of lawyers—serious men and women who counselled her with care, who tried to make sure she understood the terms of the contract she was entering into. She tried. She really tried.

'No further call on the crown. After divorce and settlement no further obligation on the part of the Prince Andreas to support you, financially or in any other way.'

That stood out like a sore thumb. Yes, she understood this. The wedding was something she'd agreed to do and then she'd get on with her life.

She felt in a daze. It was as if that one small drink Georgiou had offered her had anaesthetized her.

She simply had to sign. She simply had to trust.

And after the signing someone took Deefer away. She knew it had to happen. 'He'll be well looked after, miss. We'll keep him safe in the kitchens until the fuss is over but he can't stay with you during the wedding.' The girl said it like a joke as she lifted Deefer from Holly's arms and Holly thought, No one's staying with me at the wedding. No one.

It was time to dress. Lace. Chiffon. Gold filigree. Hoops and flounces.

No bustles. No bows. Not that she was noticing. She felt like a puppet, pulled around at will, dressed at will. There were women everywhere, fussing about her clothes, even down to the exquisite underwear they produced with the dress. Manicurists. Make-up artists. Hair consultants. All plural. One finger each, she wanted to say to the manicurists, but she was beyond joking.

She felt like a slave in a harem. Being primped and painted for the royal master.

And then it was time. The doors swung open and liveried footmen stood ready to escort her to the chapel.

'Holly?'

She looked past the footmen. There was Tia Karedes, Queen of Aristo. Dressed exquisitely in silver brocade, looking a million dollars.

'You look lovely, my dear,' Tia said softly. 'But I wondered… would you like Sebastian to give you away?'

'Sebastian?'

'By rights he should stand by Andreas,' Tia said diffidently. 'But seeing that Sebastian has ordered this marriage I've said to him that the very least he can do is give you an arm to lean on. If I'm right and you need one.'

Did she need one? She was standing in the centre of the room, surrounded by servants, a vision of what a royal bride looked like. She felt so far out of her skin she might well be in outer space.

Tia was offering her the Crown Prince's arm to support her as she went to this mock marriage.

Any arm at all, she thought blindly. So much for going into this all guns blazing. Her courage was somewhere below her elegantly shod toes.

'Yes, please,' she whispered. 'And thank you for offering. I suspect I need any arm I can get.'

* * *

He hadn't seen her for three days and he'd forgotten…or maybe he'd never known…that she could look like this.

Of course he'd never known she could look like this. A royal bride.

She was an ethereal vision, a confection of antique lace and satin. Her dress was superbly crafted to show the full swell of her breasts. Antique lace clung to each lovely curve. No bustles, he thought with approval as he watched her enter the chapel. No bows. He'd stipulated that, and the royal seamstresses had taken him at his word, but beyond that they'd indulged in every last fantasy to create a truly royal bride.

She was every inch a bride, every inch of her arranged as it should be, so she stood like Cinderella making her entrance to the ball. She was beautiful enough to take a man's breath away. She was beautiful enough to entrance a prince…

His brother was surely entranced. The king-in-waiting stood by her side, waiting for the music to cue their slow steps along the aisle. Sebastian was in full regimentals, black and gold and crimson. This ceremony was designed to show the country that the royal family was not ashamed of this connection. This was a righting of past wrongs but it was being done with all the pomp and splendour they could muster.

Sebastian had been looking down at the girl on his arm as the chapel doors swung open, but now his gaze turned to his brother standing at the end of the aisle. What have we here? his gaze said. What am I doing, bringing beauty to you?

It was as much as Andreas could do not to walk forward and punch his lights out. That his brother touch her…

Yet this was his brother's attempt to do the right thing. What was wrong with him that he object?

It was just… He didn't want Holly to have anything to do with Sebastian. He didn't want Holly to have anything to do with the royal family.

She was wearing one of the family tiaras. His mother must have lent it to her. He flashed a glance at Tia and saw his mother's warm glance of approval.

They'd approved when he'd married Christina. If he'd brought Holly home when he should have brought her home...

This was out of kilter. Time out of frame.

Holly looked scared to death.

The background music faded. The royal trumpeter sounded forth, a single high call. The traditional bridal march for a royal.

The congregation stood. The royal household. Political dignitaries. All those who'd been deemed essential to be here.

Sebastian's hand pressed Holly's and she started the long walk towards him. Her face was parchment white, devoid of expression. It was almost as if Sebastian was pressuring her forward.

There was a murmur from those around them. His captive bride, being led to the slaughter.

'Stop,' he said and the congregation gasped as one.

Was he mad? Doing this at such a time?

But he wasn't mad. He knew exactly what had to be done regardless of who was watching. Before he could let any more doubt creep in he left the waiting priest and strode swiftly down the long aisle to meet his bride.

She looked up at him, dazed. Seemingly numb.

'Leave her, Sebastian,' he said, and when Sebastian opened his mouth to argue he fixed him with a look that might, in a bygone age, have seen his head on a block. To give such a look to his future king... But Sebastian was his brother and was, this day, of little import compared to the girl on his arm.

And Sebastian had the sense to see it. He gave his brother a quizzical smile and stepped back. The trumpeter's notes faded into an uncertain murmur and then ceased altogether.

'You look frightened,' Andreas said and he took her hands in his and waited until she found the courage to look up at him.

'N...no.'

'Liar.'

'Just overwhelmed,' she managed.

'Then don't be,' he said, speaking to her and only to her

'his is between you and me. A marriage between us. And I'm
ily Andreas, the boy you once loved.'

Who knew what those around were thinking? He couldn't
are. All he knew was that these few minutes were all he had
convince her to go through with this; not to bolt and run, but
either to submit in fear.

'With a bold heart or not at all,' he whispered, and she
oked up at him as if he were a stranger.

'A bold heart...'

'You were never a coward, Holly,' he said. 'You can ride a
ilf-broken horse bareback. You can take down a steer. You can
de muster at dawn with any man. Surely you can find it in
our heart to take me on as well.'

There was a ripple of laughter through the chapel. This
ight be unconventional but it was romantic and even the
liticians were smiling.

'I'm not afraid of you,' she whispered.

'Then what, my heart?'

'I...'

'You want more time?'

That shocked her. Her eyes widened. She gazed at him, and
en she looked around the chapel where the who's who of
risto were assembled waiting to see her marry.

And suddenly her smile was back, a glimmer at first, and
en a full-on grin. 'What, you're offering me five minutes?'

'Take six if you want.'

'You're all heart.'

'You want to get married?' he said. 'We're ready and waiting.'

'You make it sound ordinary.' The whole congregation
uld hear but neither of them were aware of it.

'People do it every day. Just because you're wearing a
ira... Take it off if it bothers you.'

'You'd marry me without the tiara?'

'I'd marry you with nothing on at all,' he said and the un-
rtain smiles around the chapel became chuckles. This wasn't
iat anyone had expected—in this atmosphere redolent of

royal history and pageantry it was almost as if a breath of fres
air had blown through the chapel.

'I reckon you wouldn't,' she said, and grinned and he coul
see the girl she'd once been; the girl she still was under the pai
and loneliness the past had thrown at her.

'I reckon I would.' His eyes were daring her, laughing wit
her. 'You want to try me?'

'I reckon not,' she whispered, but the tension was gon
He'd won, he thought. She was looking at him the way she'
looked at him all those years ago. As if he was just Andrea
Just a boy.

A boy to his girl. A man to his woman.

A bride to his groom.

'With this ring I thee wed…'

He slipped the band of gold on her finger and she looke
down at it and then looked at the man facing her. Andreas.

She'd dreamed of this moment. It had always been a girl
romantic longing. Her Cinderella moment. Marrying h
prince. And here she was, doing it for real.

Yet it was all fake. She was doing it for the sake of h
country. The marriage would end and she'd go on as before

Not as before. She stared at the wedding band, at Andreas
strong fingers as he settled it in place, and then she looked
into his face.

Her husband.

She meant these vows.

Okay, this marriage might only last a few weeks but it w
all she had. She'd waited for ten long years and here she wa
hesitating, acting like a wilting violet. Making him talk h
down the aisle. Responding to his vows with whispers.

She was no timid virgin and this was her husband. If sl
only had weeks…she'd go back to Munwannay and the
memories would have to last for the rest of her life.

This had all been one-sided. She'd submitted to everythin
On the middle finger of her right hand she wore her father

ring. It was a rough-cast band of gold that had been wrought from gold found on Munwannay. The seam had never amounted to anything but she could still remember the excitement when it had been found.

'We'll be rich,' her father had exulted, swinging her round and round the kitchen in dizzy excitement. 'I'll be able to give you and your mother everything you want.'

He'd had two rings cast—wedding rings to cement the future. Heaven knew what her mother had done with hers—probably cast it away with the marriage—but her father had worn his until he died.

And now…

The priest was about to go on, assuming there was one ring only. But before he could do so, she'd tugged it off and handed it over.

'Bless this,' she whispered. 'And then wear it, Andreas.'

She'd caught him by surprise. He'd never worn a wedding ring—there was no indent around his ring finger to say he'd worn a ring during his marriage to Christina.

For a moment she thought he'd refuse. She met his gaze, steadily, her look a challenge. Come on, this is under my terms as well.

His lips quirked into a glimmer of a smile.

'Well, then,' the priest said and there was a faint trace of relief in his voice. He took Holly's ring and blessed it.

'With this ring I thee wed.'

And then there was the party.

At what point had she stopped being the wilting bride? Andreas moved among the wedding guests and his gaze kept turning to his bride, over and over again.

She was talking and laughing and moving among the guests as if she were born to the occasion. Munwannay had always been a social hub and she'd been bred to society. He knew that, but he hadn't expected this. The guest list meant that he had to do the expected. There were so many people who'd be offended if he slighted them today. So he couldn't hold her tight to him; he had to work the crowd alone. He'd warned his family to look out for her; to protect her as much as they could, but it seemed Holly needed no protection.

She spoke his language almost perfectly. Her fluency stunned him. Yes, she'd learned it as a kid, as a shared intimacy with him, but that she'd kept it up…

She joked, she laughed, she seemed genuinely interested in those around her. She was working the crowd as much as he was.

Their people loved her. The crazy, intimate scene in the church had disarmed everyone who saw it and now she was taking full advantage of the good humour she'd engendered.

He saw Sebastian watching her from the sidelines and saw his brother's dark eyes crease in admiration. And something else.

He'd been talking to a politician, an officious little man who was congratulating him on his choice of wife. 'We were so concerned. Another scandal would have undone us all, yet you've turned the thing around.'

But when he saw Sebastian watching his bride, it was Andreas who turned around, apologizing brusquely and heading through the crowd to Holly's side. It was the way Sebastian had looked at her. She was an innocent.

No. She was his wife.

The knowledge was like a blast of light through fog, an unbelievable fact that would disappear any moment. But for now…

'Holly,' he said and slipped his arm round her waist in a gesture that was entirely proprietary.

'Hi,' she said and snuggled up against him in a gesture that was entirely unroyal. 'Having fun?'

'I don't do fun,' he said without thinking, and she frowned. 'What, never?'

'This is work.'

'No, but there are some really nice people here.' She sighed. 'I'm doing all my talking for the next fifty years. I'll remember this back at Munwannay. What are we drinking?'

He looked at the glass she was holding—golden bubbles. 'French champagne.'

'I like it,' she said. 'I think I need more.'

'Right now?'

'Maybe not. A tipsy bride is not a good look. Do you think I can sneak away and check on Deefer?'

'He's in very good hands.'

'Yes, but they're not my hands. How long do wedding receptions last?'

'Until the bride and groom leave.'

She brightened. 'Hey, that's us, right? So can we leave?'

Tia was suddenly there. His mother. She'd kept things under control since her husband died. If it weren't for Tia…well, maybe the monarchy would have disintegrated long since, he thought. She was always where she was needed. Now she touched her son on his shoulder.

'The older people need to leave. So, therefore, do you.'

'That's just what Holly's been saying.'

'She's a wise child.' Tia smiled her approval at Holly. 'You've done very well, dear.'

Holly flushed. 'I…thank you…'

'For a captive bride,' Andreas said without thinking, and he saw the flash of surprise that said she'd forgotten. For the moment.

But she suppressed it. The twinkle appeared again. 'He gave me a dog,' she told Tia, as if that explained everything.

'He always was a kind boy,' Tia said.

'Kind, huh?' Holly said, and gave him a look that almost had him blushing.

But Tia was into organizational mode. She wasn't looking for nuances. 'You know the people who need to be formally farewelled,' she told Andreas. 'The two of you do the rounds. Quickly though, or it'll be said we slighted someone.'

'We can't split up and do 'em faster?' Holly asked.

'You don't know who…'

'I'm figuring it out,' Holly said. 'I've been watching. My mother brought me up on social nuances. I'm thinking I could point to every person here who's likely to take offence. But you're right, of course, I can't be depended on and I really need to see my dog. Okay, my husband. Let's get this lot farewelled so we can get on with our lives.'

It felt like an order. He felt…bossed. Holly moved through the dignitaries like a professional. As he steered her from person to person she greeted them with her hands outstretched, a royal bride receiving the attention she deserved.

She could do this, he thought with a shock. He glanced aside at his mother and saw her watching Holly and thought it wasn't just him and his pride in her. She could be royal.

There was another shock, a smack in the solar plexus that went right along with the strange feel of the ring on his finger. If he'd married her ten years ago…

Right, as if that could have happened. When his father had been alive—no way. But now… He glanced further across the crowded reception room and there was Sebastian, still watching her. Smiling.

Royal approval, or simply Sebastian's habitual reaction to a beautiful woman?

But if Sebastian approved… What had happened in the church today had changed things. Holly had become a real person to the country—a real princess?

Could they have a real marriage?

The thought was mind-blasting. It made his arm tighten on Holly's waist so she looked up at him enquiringly. 'Andreas?'

'It's time we went,' he managed.

'Yes, dear,' she said and they were such a domestic couple of words that they made him blink. Then she smiled and the heat in his body kept right on building.

They had to go. He had to take her…away.

His wife.

CHAPTER EIGHT

SHE hadn't counted on being dumped unceremoniously in the kitchen with Deefer, but that was exactly what happened.

The crowd parted as Andreas left with his wife. At the last minute he swept her up in his arms and they left behind a crowd cheering and wishing them the best. She lay submissive in his arms—what else was a bride to do, after all? But then instead of carrying her triumphantly up the grand central staircase to the royal bridal chamber—or wherever palaces accommodated newlyweds—he shoved door after door open, carrying her down into the rear of the castle to the servants' quarters. Finally he swung open a last door and set her on her feet.

She almost staggered. The dress was a dead weight around her—she'd been carrying half a ton all day. She'd been too dazed to notice. When Andreas in his fabulous royal regalia was carrying her she didn't care, but set down unceremoniously in the royal kitchen she found she did care. A lot.

The kitchen had vast, ancient flagstones, a range that took up half a wall, a table that could seat twenty or so—and little else. It was deserted, apart from Deefer who peered sleepily from a dog bed by the stove, gave his tail a perfunctory wag and then finally decided it did behove him to raise himself to welcome his mistress.

She bent to greet him and Andreas was already backing out the door. What the…?

'Um…is the Cinderella thing over?' she asked uncertainly. 'Is it midnight yet? My gown's still a gown.'

'Stay here,' he growled. 'I didn't expect… I have things to organize.'

'You didn't expect what?' she demanded.

'A wife,' he said and paused, stepped forward, hauled her close and kissed her. One harsh, demanding and possessive kiss—and then he was gone. 'Wait,' he said over his shoulder as he strode away down the corridor. 'Go nowhere.'

And where was a girl to go after that? Nowhere. Even if she could find her way back to her apartments through the corridors. Which she couldn't.

So she sat by the stove in her ridiculous bridal gear and waited for her husband and tried to make herself think of something other than how she was married and she didn't know what was going to happen and she was…scared?

Scared of something happening?

Um…no. Scared of something not happening.

What would happen if someone came in and found her here? The servants would come eventually, she thought. There she'd be when they came in to cook breakfast, the royal bride hugging her dog, looking ridiculous.

'We're in over our heads,' she told Deefer, but Deefer was one tired pup and he simply curled up into a ball on the crazy lace confection covering her knees and slept again.

Lucky Deefer.

Fifteen minutes. Twenty. The clock over the vast mantel ticked like a bomb. Tick tick tick.

She was going nuts.

The door swung open again. Andreas. Still in his ceremonial bridal toggery. Still looking absurdly handsome.

Still her husband.

'We're ready,' he said and she suddenly had a ghastly vision of the royal brides she'd heard of in history—a dozen witnesses clustered around the bed waiting for evidence of her virginity.

'Um…we?' she whispered, and he chuckled and strode forward, lifted Deefer from her arms and pulled her lightly up to stand beside him.

'Georgiou.'

'Oh, goody,' she whispered. 'My favourite person.'

'My favourite helicopter pilot,' he said. 'I've had too much wine to fly myself. Not that I'm drunk but there's zero alcohol tolerance for flying. Besides, I wish to concentrate entirely on my bride. So what say Georgiou takes us away from all this? Back to our island.'

Her eyes widened in shock. 'We can just…go?'

'That's just what I think we should do,' he said. 'We've done the honourable thing, my love. The rest of the night's just for us.'

'And Georgiou.'

'As you say,' he said and grinned. 'But I'm thinking the island's big enough for all of us.'

This was ridiculous. She should have insisted on changing clothes, Holly thought as she sat on the opposite side of the helicopter to Andreas and hugged Deefer. To travel in her wedding gown—she still had the tiara in her curls!—seemed crazy. As did the fact that Andreas was still wearing his royal regalia. He was leaning back in the luxurious leather chair that served as the helicopter seat, his eyes almost closed, as if in meditation. What was he thinking?

He had a bride?

What was he going to do with her?

In days of old she'd be a trembling virgin, terrified of what lay ahead. Bolstered by maternal advice… Don't be frightened, there's nothing to it. Lie back and think of England and it'll soon be over.

She bit back a nervous giggle and Andreas turned.

'So what are you thinking?'

'Of England,' she said and bit her bottom lip and thought the tension was going to kill her. What was she doing? A kid from Munwannay, in the royal helicopter, in full bridal toggery, being carried to an island hideaway with her prince.

Her husband.

If he thought he was going to…

Of course he thought he was going to, she told herself. He'd gone to all this trouble to get them alone. And they were married, in the sight of God and before such a congregation…

'England,' he said blankly.

'It's what all brides think of on their wedding night.'

'Really?'

'Absolutely,' she assured him, trying hard not to sound breathless. 'I'm trying to sort out the English mountains. Ben something… Isn't that the biggest? And what's the capital of Sussex? Don't distract me.'

He didn't distract her. He simply grinned, turned back to his window and let her be. By the time they landed she'd not only had time to think about England's biggest mountain, but she'd had time to reach a point where her nerves were threatening to snap. What did she think she was doing? She hadn't agreed to this. It was a marriage in name only.

No. It wasn't. Not when Andreas looked as he did, when she felt as she did and it had been ten long years. Holly's life on a remote cattle station had been very remote indeed. In a few weeks she'd be back there and this was all she'd have to remember.

Except… Except…

'I can't get pregnant,' she said suddenly into the stillness as the helicopter landed and the roar of the motor died to nothing. The thought had hit her as a vicious slap. What was she risking? The whole nightmare happening all over again?

'It won't happen,' Andreas said gravely.

'I believe that's what you said last time.'

'I've taken precautions.'

'Like you've had a vasectomy?'

He smiled, but the smile didn't reach his eyes. 'No,' he said, 'though Christina wanted me to.'

'Your wife wanted you to have a vasectomy?'

'She didn't want children.'

'Did you want children?'

'More than anything in the world,' he said simply and she knew he was speaking a fundamental truth. 'But you needn't worry. Not with you. Not this night.'

'So you've brought the odd condom.'

'Or six,' he said and the gravity went from his eyes. 'Or more if we need.'

'You're acting on a huge presumption.'

'Which is?'

'That I'll go to bed with you.'

'You put your ring on my finger.'

'So that means…'

'You want me as much as I want you.'

'Andreas, you and I…'

'I understand,' he said softly. 'No, Holly, I'm not asking you to join the royal entourage. I will keep my word and let you go. But for tonight… I'm hoping tonight can just be for us. A night out of frame. So I've brought you here.'

'And I've come,' she whispered. 'But, Andreas, if I were to get pregnant…'

'I'd take care of it this time,' he said, strongly. 'I'd take care of you.'

'You'd take care of…it?' The joy had gone out of the night. Reality, cold, hard, appalling, had raised its ugly head. This wasn't a fairy tale. This was real.

He'd take care of…it? What, abortion?

'I'll do nothing you don't want,' he said.

'Like I believe that. Bringing me all this way…'

'I'll take no unwilling bride to bed,' he said, sounding suddenly stern. Royal even, and the thought almost made her smile. He might be her Andreas, the Andreas she loved with all her heart, but try as he might, he was still a prince. Her prince.

'It's not that I'm unwilling, Andreas,' she whispered, trying to make him see. 'God help me, I've wanted you for years.'

'That's wonderful,' he said, and he smiled that gut-wrenching smile she loved so much.

'But there are consequences,' she managed.

'There are,' he said gravely. They were strapped into separate seats, separated by three feet of open space. He reached across and touched her hand, fleetingly, a feather touch of something that was obviously supposed to be reassurance. And stupidly, insensibly she was reassured.

But not enough. Not enough.

'It'd be crazy to go to bed,' she said miserably. 'When this marriage is only for a few weeks.'

'The marriage is for as long as we want it to be,' he said.

'Right. You need a commoner for a bride like you need the plague, and I need to go home.'

'Do you really need to go home?'

'Yes,' she whispered, thinking back to that tiny grave.

I'll take care of it. The words had brought Adam's loss flooding back. Her mother, visiting her fleetingly, saying 'Never mind, dear. He was never going to marry you. Losing *it* is for the best. Now you can get on with your life.'

She'd never got on with her life. She'd worked hard, she'd tried to live her life to the full, but a part of her had been buried the night she'd buried Adam. To get it back...

'This is wrong,' she whispered, miserably, and Andreas reached out again and took her hand strongly in his.

'It isn't wrong,' he said. 'Not now. But we'll take this as it comes. Don't look like that, my love. I will *not* force myself on you.'

'But you've brought six condoms.'

'Just in case,' he said and he quizzed her gently with his teasing smile. 'Just on the chance you decide I'm not so bad after all. I *am* your husband, Holly.'

'You're saying you have rights?'

'No rights,' he said. 'Let's just play this night as it comes.'

Okay. She wasn't going to sleep with him. That was the sensible course, and she knew enough of her...her husband...to know he wouldn't take her against her will.

So it was only her will that was the problem, she thought, and her will had to be cast-iron. She'd walk into the pavilion from the helicopter, she'd bid Andreas a civil goodnight—maybe she'd even apologize because just possibly she'd given him the wrong idea—and then she'd go to bed. In her bedroom. With the door locked.

Sophia would be here. That steadied her. She could do this.

But there was the first hiccup in her plans. The pavilion was deserted. There was no Sophia and Nikos to meet them. Georgiou escorted them to the entrance from the helicopter pad and then faded into the darkness. Wherever the staff were tonight they weren't here. It was Andreas himself who flung open the huge doors—and when she saw what was inside Holly gasped in shock.

Candles. Candles as far as the eye could see.

The huge central courtyard with its magnificent pool was a glittering mass of flickering candlelight. There were even tiny tealights floating on the water of the pool, their flames reflecting over and over in the depths of the still water.

The fireflies were at work as well, seemingly encouraged by such a mass of flickering light. Last time she'd been here she'd seen and loved them, but there surely hadn't been as many as there were this night. Their tiny moving glows brought the whole place alive with light, alive with the warmth of the flames.

'So many fireflies,' she whispered.

'I paid 'em to come,' Andreas said and looked smug.

What else had he paid to have done?

The big table had been removed. There was one small table right by the water, set for two. A path of candles led to it.

Right by the door—in a pool of light created by a sweep of graded candles—was a pile of pillows. Huge. Soft.

In the middle of the central pillow was a bone. One vast marrowbone, with a central section carefully carved out so a small dog could reach the marrow. If he tried hard enough. If he didn't succumb to the pure luxury of the down-filled cushions beforehand.

'You're even trying to seduce my dog,' she whispered, awed, as Andreas took the sleepy Deefer from her arms and plopped him on the pillows. Deefer looked adoringly up at Andreas as if to say if this was seduction then thank you very much, he'd take it every time. He put his small mouth round his very big bone, he snuggled into the cushions, he put two paws possessively over the bone—and he went back to sleep. Clearly he was in doggy heaven and he intended to stay there for a very long time.

'I don't think I had to try very hard,' Andreas said and smiled. 'I suspect Deefer considers himself seduced. And now, my love,' he growled and took her by the waist. 'Now for us.'

'Andreas…'

'Meal only,' he said, sounding innocent. 'I swear.'

'When did you set this all up?' she whispered, awed.

'I didn't.' His dark eyes gleamed in appreciation as he surveyed the scene beforehand. 'I'd anticipated spending this night at the palace. Only then…it seemed important. So I rang Sophia and said we'd be here.'

Sophia must have done all this before, Holly thought, trying not to think it, but thinking it all the same.

'She hasn't done it before,' Andreas growled, his hold on her tightening.

'How did you know…?'

'I could feel it. Holly, despite how this appears, this is no practised seduction scene.'

'N…no?'

'I brought Christina here early in our marriage,' he said. 'Years ago. She loathed it. No shops. No jet-setting friends. She never came again and I brought no one else.'

'You've never brought a woman here?' she demanded, not believing him. 'Don't tell me there was only Christina.'

'I won't tell you that. I won't lie to you,' he said. 'But I've brought none of my mistresses here. Until you.'

'I'm not your mistress,' she said sharply and he nodded, as if in courteous acknowledgement.

'Maybe that's why you're here. You're my wife,' he said and his hold on her tightened, until suddenly it seemed that tight wasn't enough, he was forced to sweep her up in his arms and hold her against his heart. 'You are my wife, and this night I intend to take you. Or…' he amended as he felt her stiffen, 'I intended to take you. Until I heard your very reasonable reservations about why six condoms won't necessarily work. But let's not worry about that now. I believe Sophia has left a meal for us. I haven't seen you eat all day. For what I have in store for you tonight I want no wilting bride.'

So they ate. To her amazement she was hungry. Sophia must have half expected this. She'd surely planned it. But still Sophia remained invisible. It was Andreas who did the serving, disappearing and appearing again like a genie producing his magic.

He was still dressed in full dress uniform, his tunic buttoned high to his throat, his scarlet sash and medals emblazoned on his chest. He'd removed his dress sword but that was his only concession to casual. His high leather boots gleamed like jet-black mirrors. And his tight-fitting pants… There should be a law against them, she thought. For a man to wear such things… For a prince to wear them as he served her…

He was a prince serving his bride. And with food fit for the bride of such a man. Course after course, each small, each tantalizing, each delicious.

Kotosoupa Avgolemono… A chicken and rice soup, with egg and lemon…

He'd made this for her before, she remembered, once when her parents had left them alone together for the evening. 'I'll cook,' he'd said, and she'd scoffed but he'd simply smiled his fabulously sexy smile and made her a soup she'd remembered ever since.

She'd watched him make it. For years after he left she'd tried to make it again, but it had never tasted the same.

It did tonight.

She raised her spoon to her mouth and he was watching every move; a hawk watching his prey, she thought.

'You like?' he said and she closed her eyes and savoured the taste of it and the memories and she couldn't lie.

'It's magic. You cooked this for me years ago…'

'I did,' he said and smiled. 'You remembered. I'll cook it for you again. Whenever you want, my heart.'

She almost choked. She looked across the table and he was smiling at her and she thought of those six condoms and she thought, No, no, no.

'Leave me alone,' she managed, sounding virtuous. 'I need to concentrate.'

'There's plenty to concentrate on,' he agreed gravely. 'You keep concentrating, my heart, and I'll keep feeding you.'

So she kept eating. There was no choice—and in truth she had been hungry.

There was no way she was leaving this table hungry. Andreas was already leaving, to return with what came next. Tiny vol au vents, made with flaky, buttery pastry that melted almost as it touched her lips, filled with ingredients she couldn't identify and didn't need to—the combination of flavours was just right. Just perfect. Tiny and exquisite.

Then there was a modest medallion of rare fillet beef, served with baby mushrooms and a rich burgundy sauce. There were slivers of young asparagus, oozing butter. A tiny pile of creamy mashed potato. With truffle? Surely not. But, yes, she'd tasted truffle once in the distant past, and here it was again, unmistakable.

They didn't talk. She couldn't talk. She was saying a mantra over and over in her head.

Sensible. Sensible. Sensible.

How could she stay sensible? She was achingly aware of his every movement, of every flicker of those dark, dark eyes. He was watching her as she ate, devouring her with his eyes. She should object. She should…

Just eat, she told herself. Just watch him. Maybe even relax a little? Just take every moment of this magic meal as it came. The time for making things clear they were going no further was for later.

The steak was gone, the plates cleared by her prince, her waiter, her husband. He poured her a glass of dessert wine, a botrytis-affected Semillon. To her amazement it was Australian, a winemaker she knew, a wine she'd loved for always.

'How…?'

'I remembered,' he said and smiled. 'I had Georgiou find this wine. Just for tonight.'

She drank and her resolutions grew hazier. This was only her second glass. She was hardly drunk. She was just…entranced?

Seduced?

No!

But he'd remembered her wine.

And then there were sweets—tiny, bite-sized eclairs oozing with rich, dark chocolate and creamy custard. There were strawberries tasting how strawberries should and never did, but this night how could they help but taste like this? Andreas watched her as she put each red fruit between her lips, and he smiled and they might as well be making love. The candles were flickering, burning to stubs. They were going out, one by one, and the light was fading.

The night was ending.

She was half expecting Sophia to appear, to clear the table, to bid them goodnight, but there was still no one in sight. Just the two of them. She and her husband.

She took her last sip of coffee. 'I need to go to bed,' she said, a little unsteadily, and Andreas was behind her, drawing out her chair, helping her to her feet, his hands holding hers with strength and desire and absolute surety of what was to follow.

'I believe we've missed our bridal waltz,' he whispered into her ear and suddenly it was all she could do not to chuckle.

'You have some set-up here.'

'I knew I built it for something. I believe I built it for tonight.'

He was whispering into her ear, his breath warm on her skin, his touch sending heat surging to every part of her body. He deliberately unfastened the top two buttons of his tunic, loosening the garment as a non-royal would shrug off a tie. Then before she could respond, before she could haul her resolutions into line again, he swept her up into his arms and strode to a central panel. Still holding her in his arms, he pushed discreet buttons and on came a waltz, slow and soft and dreamy.

Wordlessly he carried her back to the side of the pool, he set her to her feet, he drew her into his arms and started to dance with her.

This was the most perfect seduction scene. And she was being perfectly seduced.

She should fight. She should push away and leave.

How could she do such a thing when Andreas was holding her in his arms?

So she danced.

With the social ambition of her parents she'd been taught to dance almost before she'd been taught to ride, but it was years since she had. Like riding a horse, though, you never forgot. And she'd never forgotten dancing with Andreas. The first night he'd arrived in Munwannay her parents had put on a dance to welcome him. He'd asked for the waltz, she'd been swept onto the floor—and her life had changed.

Not one thing had changed since then, she thought dazedly. She was falling in love all over again. She was being swept around the floor with her lovely bridal gown looped up and held, the rich folds of silk swaying around her. Andreas's arms were holding her as if she were the most precious porcelain; as if she was the most desirable woman in the world.

As he was her most desirable man. Her prince.

She was melting into him. Her face was against his breast. His opened tunic meant that her face was brushing his chest. He felt…irresistible. He smelled irresistible. Strong and male and…her husband.

No. This wasn't sensible. This marriage was for a few weeks only and if something happened…

But she wanted him so badly it was like a searing, physical ache. A void that had to be filled and only he could fill it. He was holding her closer, closer. Their feet moved in perfect unison; he was anticipating her every move, or maybe she was anticipating his. Who knew?

Her husband.

'Andreas,' she whispered and she heard him groan softly into her hair.

'My love?'

'Enough already with the seduction scene,' she whispered unsteadily.

'You don't like it?'

'I said I've had it with the set-up,' she whispered back and her hands came up and gripped his head and tugged his face down so his mouth met hers. 'I can't wait. Damn the risks. Oh, Andreas, I know this is crazy, but I want you so much.'

'I wanted you to want me,' he said, and she could practically see his smile.

She gave a little gasp and pulled away. He was laughing. Laughing! With those dark, dark eyes that glowed with desire.

'And do you want me to want you?' he asked, and suddenly the laughter was gone. The look in his eyes was deadly serious. 'Holly, I've said I'll take no unwilling bride. I want you more than life itself but you come to me willingly or not at all. Do you want me as much as I want you?'

And there was only one answer she could give. There was only one answer in the world. Sensible or not.

It wasn't sensible. It was dumb, dumb, dumb but she didn't care.

'I do,' she said simply, and then gasped as he swept her up into his arms again. And then there was no room for anything. There was no room for any words at all.

* * *

The night was warm and starlit. His bedroom was open to the night, the shutters pushed far back so it seemed that his vast bed was on a platform overlooking the moonlit sea. He carried her there triumphantly, tenderly, and she lay back in his arms and smiled up at him and thought, this is where I should be. This is my husband. This is my heart, my home.

My Andreas.

There was no going back now. He was setting her down by the bed and she could barely stand. Her body was on fire and if he'd put her away she would have fought her way back to him. He was hers. Her body was aching for him, throbbing its want. She gazed up at him and saw her hot, desperate need reflected in the eyes of the man she loved.

Andreas.

'Holly,' he whispered, his voice husky with passion. 'My wife.'

And then… How was she suddenly without clothes? How was she so soon lying on silken sheets with nothing between herself and the man she loved but sheer, raw desire?

Had he undressed her? He must have, while she was concentrating on ridding him of unwanted garments. But she hardly saw his clothes. All she thought of was his body. All she wanted was him. Years ago she'd known and gloried in this man's body and tonight it felt as if she was coming home.

'You're beautiful,' she whispered, awed, as they sank onto the bed together, and he laughed, a soft, throaty chuckle as he laid her on the silken sheets, following her down and gathering her naked body into his arms.

'You… To say that to me, my heart…'

And then he was kissing her, not just on the lips but everywhere, toes to forehead and back down again, slowly, tenderly, while she writhed and moaned with pleasure. She was alive under his hands, under his touch. Her body felt as if it were waking after a long, long sleep, every nerve-end aware, alight, afire.

She was touching him too, running her hands through his

hair, feeling his nakedness, glorying in the hard arrant maleness of his body. She was alive as she hadn't been alive for long, barren years, awaking after a too-long sleep to this all-consuming blaze. Her body was melting into him with a fierce heat she'd forgotten she was capable of feeling. The touch of him... He was hers. Hers, she thought fiercely.

For years she'd thought it was a fairy tale. She'd thought her memories of the way Andreas had made her feel were a figment of a girl's romantic yearning; her first love with a prince, a time out of frame, the full fairy story.

There'd been the odd guy she could have started something with. Neighbours. Stock and station agents. Other teachers. But she'd looked at them and internally she'd lined them up against Andreas and thought, who was she kidding? She'd had the romantic fairy tale and to go back to the real world seemed impossible.

So she'd hung onto a fairy tale, knowing it was just that, imagination and nostalgia.

Only it wasn't. For the way Andreas made her feel...

He was everything she remembered and more. Demanding, aristocratic, overwhelming in his sheer masculinity. But still tender at core, wanting her to share his exultation—no, demanding that she share his exultation. He gloried in her body, tasting her, touching her, exploring every inch of her with wonder and languorous pleasure and wanton delight—but he expected the same of her. That she know him as he wished to know her. That she give pleasure as he intended to give pleasure. That she take this coupling slowly, savouring every last moment of its wonder.

And she did. She did. The feel of his body in her arms was close to overwhelming.

And when finally, blissfully the moment came when he was entering her...taking her, demanding she follow where he led...she felt herself cry out with sheer joy. They merged, and the night exploded in a mist of white-hot desire. And then they lay, sated but still linked, still loving, until the heat built again and raw need took over from the blissful afterglow of consummation.

For this was no one-coupling night. It was as if their bodies were demanding that they make up, in part, for all these years they'd missed. This night was too precious for sleep. She'd dreamed of this man for ever and sleep was for the barren years, for another time, something to be put away as irrelevant.

All that mattered now was Andreas.

He'd changed, she thought wonderingly during this long, languorous night. His was no longer a boy's body, but a man's, hard and muscular. Royal or not, this wasn't the indulged body of a playboy prince. He'd loved working on the farm, she remembered, savouring the hard physical requirements of axing tree stumps, of hauling out rotten fence posts, of heaving bales of hay for hungry cattle. Somewhere in the last years he must have found an alternative to farm work, for his body was all muscle, hard and sinewy and fabulous.

Fabulous. The word whispered over and over in her mind as she lay with him through the night, her fingers exploring, her tongue discovering, her legs holding him possessively in between couplings. Skin against skin on the silken sheets of Andreas's vast princely bed, still they weren't close enough.

But they could be. Over and over, each time striving to be closer, closer. The night wasn't long enough. By rights they should be exhausted but there was no way this night could end with them asleep.

'You're so much more beautiful than I remembered,' he whispered, awed, at some time during the night and she thought, so are you, so are you. 'My beautiful Holly. My magical outback princess.'

Like young lovers they clung, holding to each other in the dark, exploring, exulting, wanting more, more, until dawn finally came, a tangerine flush appearing softly over the horizon, and a kind of peace that was deeper than she'd ever felt before fell over the pair of them. They lay naked and entwined and she felt seventeen again, beloved, with the world at her feet, her prince in love with her, her man in her arms and nothing could go wrong with her world ever again.

'Can I take you for a swim, my love?' Andreas whispered into the dawn, and she thought she must be dreaming.

'I believe you can take me wherever you want,' she managed.

He smiled, then swung himself up and over her, so he was smiling down at her. He kissed her on the tip of her nose. 'Then a swim it is.'

'I don't believe I'm capable of moving the tip of my smallest finger,' she whispered, cautious.

'But you'd like a swim?'

'Maybe a soak?' she whispered, tugging him back down to her.

'Then a soak you shall have,' he said, and before she knew what he was about he'd rolled off the bed and swung her up into his arms. She gave a squeak of surprise and he grinned down at her, his smile pure mischief. And then he was striding towards the door and she was too stunned to even struggle.

'We're naked,' she managed and her voice came out an even higher squeak.

'Are we?' He stopped dead, as if such a thought hadn't occurred to him. He looked down at her, and his dark eyes gleamed with laughter. 'So we are,' he said on a note of wonder. 'How wonderful.' He kissed her on the top of her head and then as she twisted he found her lips and kissed her more deeply still. But he'd reached the door and pushed the handle down with his elbow, and was striding out. Past the pool. Through the entrance hall. Out into daylight, to the open world where the beach lay before them in gold and turquoise wonder.

'Andreas, we're naked,' she squeaked again, half laughing, half shocked. The feel of his bare skin against hers in the warm morning wind was almost unbearably erotic. But she had to be sensible. Someone had to be sensible. Dear God, he was gorgeous. Her big, naked prince. Her Andreas.

Her husband.

But: 'Sophia…' she whispered desperately. 'Georgiou…'

'Sophia will have the others carefully on the other side of the pavilion,' he said, not breaking stride.

'She has instructions for when you bring your women here?'

He stopped at that. Stopped dead and his brow snapped down into a frown. 'No,' he said, and his tone was suddenly harsh. 'I've told you. I've brought no other women here.'

'Like I believe that.'

'You can believe it,' he whispered and kissed her again, so deeply there was no room for argument; there was no room for anything but heat and want and now. 'I've brought you here, my woman. My wife. It was time to bring you home.'

And then he didn't stop until he reached the shallows. He laid her down, almost reverently, on the soft sand, where the tiny waves rippled in and out. She gasped as her overheated body met the cool of the water, but then Andreas was following her down, gathering her to him, taking her to him with a desire that said this was to be no gentle soak.

'I thought…'

'You think what you like,' he growled and pulled her to him, under him, his knees sinking into the soft sand, his hands holding her face as he tugged her closer, closer until once more their bodies met, fused, merged. 'I can't think at all. My Holly. *Agapi mou*. My heart.'

CHAPTER NINE

THE following days were a dream. A honeymoon. Six condoms? There were more where they came from and it was just as well.

For once started it was impossible to stop. Holly was just as crazy as she'd been when she was seventeen, and just as helpless. She was just as hopelessly in love.

Andreas just had to look at her and she melted. He just had to touch her and every fibre of her being responded with pure, white want.

'My hot woman,' he called her, tugging her into his arms over and over. 'My captive wife. I have a mind to keep you here for ever.'

That was fine by her, she thought dreamily as the days wore on. Her time with Andreas in the past had been stolen moments, passion laced with guilt. Caution had made her hesitate on her wedding night, but having abandoned caution she discovered there was nothing more to worry about. There was nothing but the love she felt for this man.

He could take her in any way he pleased, and he did, he did. In turn she took him. He might be aristocratically demanding, but so too could she be. He could be tender in turn and he brought out a gentleness in her she didn't know she had.

Sophia appeared again, and Nikos and Georgiou, but they stayed in the background. This was their own desert island, their own paradise, just for them.

Deefer was a part of their world, a bouncing ball of fun, flying along the beach, rounding up gulls, following them bravely into the surf, but collapsing in true puppy fashion, exhausted and happy while his master and mistress took their pleasure until they, too, felt the same.

Paradise, just for them.

Only of course it couldn't last. They were given three days and then the fairy tale ended.

It ended with a knock on the bedroom door. It was eleven in the morning. They'd swum and made love lazily in the shallows, then wandered back hand in hand for a late breakfast by the pool. While Deefer slept the sleep of a truly contented pup, Andreas and Holly had showered with the intent of dressing. But that was as far as they'd got. Their bed was too inviting.

Now they lay coiled together in the aftermath of loving, hazy with heat and spent passion. But the knock sounded urgent. Andreas swore, shifted Holly in his arms and called, 'What is it?'

'His Majesty, Prince Sebastian, is on the phone for you.' It was Georgiou, sounding, for Georgiou, apologetic.

'Damn.' Andreas moved Holly gently away from him, kissing her lightly on the forehead. 'If I go will you promise to stay?'

'You think I have energy to move? Don't be long.'

'If my brother calls…' He didn't finish. He hauled on his clothes and disappeared and Holly was left with vague forebodings.

Her forebodings were right. Andreas was gone for half an hour. She showered again and this time she dressed, simply in a soft sarong. She tugged her hair back into a coil and fastened it and slipped her feet into sandals. She was about to emerge when he reappeared.

One look at his face told her their idyll was over.

'We need to go,' he told her and her heart sank. His face was set and hard, already moving forward.

'Back to the mainland?'

'I need to go to Greece,' he told her. 'There are rumours that the missing diamond's been sold to a private buyer. The royals from Calista are sniffing around already. If they find it before we do…' He left the sentence unfinished but he was already moving towards the bathroom. 'Georgiou's checking the helicopter now. We're leaving in half an hour.'

And that was that. No 'can you be ready?' No 'I'm sorry the honeymoon's been interrupted.' Andreas was moving on.

Back to being a royal. And that left her…where?

He was stripping, stepping into the shower again. He wouldn't want to smell of lovemaking when he met his family, she thought dully. He'd need to be royal again.

She swallowed. Maybe she could stay here.

She couldn't. She knew that. She needed to go back to the mainland. For a start. To see… If there was a future there for her?

But Andreas had never said there was a future for her as a princess. As his wife. As far as Andreas was concerned she still wanted to go home.

Of course she did, she reminded herself sharply. Of course she did.

She left him showering. Sophia was waiting outside, looking anxious. 'What will you do?' she asked.

'What comes next,' Holly whispered. 'In truth, Sophia, I don't know. But for now… I have so few clothes and I'm about to return to Aristo as a royal wife. Let's you and I do a fast sort through this appalling wardrobe and see if we can find something that makes me look vaguely respectable.'

'More than respectable,' Sophia said and hugged her. 'You want a wardrobe that makes you look royal. You want a wardrobe that makes Andreas wish to keep you.'

'Yeah, well that'd be a magic wardrobe,' Holly said stiffly. 'Let's not count on miracles here.'

Andreas stood under the streaming water and felt ill. He'd almost forgotten. The last three days had been a magic time out, but Sebastian's phone call had been curt to the point of being brutal. A reality check in the worst possible way.

'You have to get back here. I can't trust many people with the knowledge of the missing diamond. You have to go to Greece and search.'

'I can't leave Holly.'

'You've done what you had to do with Holly. That problem's over. Forget her. We have bigger problems now.'

'She's my wife…'

'Because she had to be your wife,' Sebastian snapped. 'You hardly want to keep her.' Then, as Sebastian heard nothing in response—heard the nuances behind Andreas's silence—he sighed. 'All right. She's beautiful, I grant you. But if you want her long term then she has to play by the rules. This situation is too complicated as it is, and if she makes it more so… Leave her on the island. Or send her back to Australia.' He hesitated. 'No. It's perhaps too soon for that. But if she sticks around, you need to make sure she stays firmly in the background.'

'She's hardly going to bring us down, Sebastian,' Andreas said.

'Anything can bring us down right now,' Sebastian answered grimly. 'We're on a knife edge. We have to find that diamond. So I want you here now.'

The phone went dead. Andreas was left staring into space. Hating it.

The royal goldfish bowl… He couldn't remember a time he hadn't hated it.

A memory popped up, uninvited and maybe untimely..

When he was six years old he'd been ill. Seriously ill, with rheumatic fever. He had glimmers of memory through a haze of fever. His huge bed with its starched white sheets, in the over-ornate hall that served as the royal nursery. Doctors surrounding him, looking grave. His mother coming into the room, sitting on his bed—an almost unheard of thing for the queen to do. His father restricted his contact with his parents to a ten-minute recital of his achievements for the day, formally performed before high tea. But this day she had stayed, and looked worried. And then he remembered the magic words—said to his nanny, Sophia.

'Very well, if that's what the doctors are ordering, you can take him home. I'll defy his father, on this. But you're not to let him forget what's due to him.'

What followed was three months in Sophia's home town, in Sophia's own home. Sophia's mountain village was known for its medicinal qualities—it was supposed to be a place where damaged lungs and hearts could find a place to heal.

Sophia had promised his father that he'd be treated as a prince, gravely and sincerely. They'd been driven to the village in one of the palace's vast limousines. Sophia had been strictly formal all the way home, but as they stood in the doorway of her home and watched the limousine disappear into the distance she'd suddenly bent and hugged him.

'I have you here, my little cabbage, and I'll make you well,' she'd said joyously. 'This is our secret but for these three months I want you to be a child. I want you to be free.'

And he had been. As his health had improved he'd swooped around the village as part of the tribe of local kids, running, playing, going to the local school, getting into mischief, falling for the misbegotten mutts that were the family pets. He'd eaten at Sophia's kitchen table with Sophia and Nikos—they'd both been granted leave of absence from the palace staff to take care of this sickly princeling.

They were sharing the rambling old house with Sophia's two grown sons and their wives, and a tribe of grandchildren. Sophia had tucked him into bed each night—a bedroom he shared with Sophia's oldest grandson. She'd hugged him and kissed him and he'd slept as he'd never slept before or since.

His mother's words had stayed with him as he returned to the palace. *You can take him home.* That was what it had felt like. He'd wanted so much to go back. His time in Australia had been a desperate attempt to relive that experience—being normal—being a kid again.

And in a way it had worked. He'd fallen in love with Holly

in the same way a six-year-old had fallen in love with Sophia. Or actually in a very different way, he thought ruefully. But there were similarities. He'd escaped into…love.

But both times had ended. Both times he'd been called back to the palace, to the place where shows of emotion were regarded as weakness. Where noise and mess, pets and mischief were not tolerated. Where the word *home* had no place. But he had no choice. It was his duty. It was his birthright.

He was needed now. He had to go back.

With Holly. It had to be with Holly.

She'd hate it, he thought. He had no right to ask this of her, even for a short while. But it was too soon to send her back to Australia.

Hell, he didn't want her back at the palace, confined to royal protocol. His fantasy with Holly had never included royal trimmings.

He looked through the open bathroom door to the bedroom beyond. Deefer was watching him from the doorway. The pup's intelligent little face was cocked to the side as if he knew his master was troubled.

'Can you be a royal dog?' he asked.

Deefer stared back at him, appearing to ponder the question. Then, bored, he gazed around him.

The bed had a massive brocade cover, tumbled now and lying half over the end of the bed. It had magnificent gold tassles on the side.

Deefer barked at the closest tassle. Then he crouched low, pounced, grabbed the tassle and headed for the main door. Dragging the priceless brocade with him.

Maybe not, Andreas thought ruefully. Maybe Deefer wasn't a royal dog as Holly wasn't a royal princess.

He closed his eyes, took a deep breath and flicked off the taps. He reached for his towel and padded through to find his clothes. A suit. Clothes to make him a prince again.

With wife? With dog?

Only if they both learned to toe the royal line.

* * *

They were on opposite sides of the helicopter again. This machine wasn't meant for lovers. Nor was it meant for man and wife.

She didn't feel like a wife right now. She was on her way to being a royal princess. She felt small and insignificant and scared.

Andreas was staring out the window to the land below. Aristo.

A reception committee was waiting. From the helicopter she could see a cluster of waiting suits, of media jostling for position.

'The press?' she asked in a small voice and Andreas sighed.

'It's only to be expected. Our marriage has caused enormous interest. However hopefully they'll back off now I've done the right thing.'

'Now I've done the right thing...'

He was still staring below. Preoccupied. How could he know that her heart felt as if it had been pierced?

'They would have had my hide if I hadn't married you,' he said grimly, almost to himself. 'It's what being a royal's all about. You're pressured from day one. Your life's not your own. Hell, if I'd been able to follow my own course... You're better out of it, Holly.'

He turned to her then and she had to fight—really fight—to get her face under control. She felt sick.

'I... How long do I need to stay?' she managed.

'I'll talk to Sebastian.'

And that was that. He'd talk to the future king. He'd do what was required.

The last three days she'd allowed herself to hope. No, she'd allowed herself to believe that there was truly a marriage, for that was what it had felt like.

I'll talk to Sebastian.

The course of their marriage was in the hands of the Prince Regent, Sebastian. Naturally.

This had been truly time out of frame, she thought dully as the helicopter landed, as the doors were hauled open to readmit the world. Three days of memories to last her for the rest of her life.

How could it be enough?

Maybe it had to be enough. They were taken over the

moment they landed. The moment the doors were open there were flashlights going everywhere, almost blinding her.

Andreas climbed out first and helped her after him. He held her hand and she clung.

She was wearing a tight-fitting, little green dress—a sundress. She should be corporate, she thought. To face this she needed power clothes. Shoulder pads. Business black.

'How was the honeymoon?' someone yelled, and there were chuckles and questions, fielded by Andreas like an expert. All she could do was cling like a limpet and hope it'd soon be over.

'How does it feel to be a royal wife?' someone called and Andreas was before her.

'Holly's not intended to be a royal wife,' he said smoothly. 'Yes, we've wed, but Holly's life is in Australia. She runs one of the most beautiful cattle stations in her country. I'll never ask her to give that up to take on royal duties.'

There was a moment's shocked hush. Then a torrent of follow-up interrogation, all of which could be summed up in the one phrase.

'You mean it's not a real marriage?

'I didn't say that,' Andreas said smoothly. 'We were married before God and we intend to keep our vows. But marriage means different things for different people. Christina and I had a royal marriage where both of us were expected to play a role in public life. But Holly's not a royal wife. To ask that of her would be unfair.'

'So you're going back to Australia?' someone demanded of her. 'When?'

'There are many things to be sorted,' Andreas interceded smoothly. 'We'll let you know.'

'But you'll attend royal functions until then?' someone called.

'She will,' Andreas said.

What was happening here? Holly thought, stunned. Limpet? Wet rag more like it. Docile bride standing meekly by her husband's side as he answered her questions. The husband as the woman's spokesperson.

'And how do I like my porridge?' she blurted out, before she could help herself.

'Pardon?' Andreas stared down at her. Everyone was staring at her.

'Tell the press how I like my porridge,' she said dangerously, and she knew no good could come of this. She could feel a wave of anger so strong it threatened to overwhelm her. But she was on the wave now and there was no way she could get off until it was ridden to its end.

'We don't understand,' a reporter complained.

'I mean if I'm asked a question—about me—then maybe I'm the one capable of answering it. I'll be going back to Australia when I feel like it,' she snapped. 'When I decide. I'm not intended for a royal wife? That sounds like I've been produced on some breeding programme. I'm sorry, my love,' she said, and she managed a saccharine smile as Andreas stared at her, astounded. 'I know. A royal wife shuts up and lets her husband speak for her. But I'm not a royal wife. You've just said so. I'm just a wife. I'm just me. Let's take that as read and move on.'

He was furious. Not just angry but almost impotent with rage. They sat in the back of the limousine on the way to the palace and he stared at her as if she'd grown two heads.

Two could play at that game. She stared right back, furiously defiant.

'A royal wife stays in the background,' he snapped.

'Does she? I wouldn't know. I'm not a royal wife.'

'Holly, you don't understand. It's imperative that our behaviour is above reproach.'

'I thought my behaviour *was* above reproach,' she said, dangerously quiet. If her father could hear her now maybe he'd warn Andreas. My daughter has a temper. Be afraid. Be very afraid.

But Andreas had no such warning. The political consequences of their actions were first and foremost in his mind and he wasn't seeing past them.

'You had a child out of wedlock,' he said tightly. 'That's enough.'

'Enough?'

'For the country to judge you. You need to be demure and quiet and respectful.'

'Respectful of you.'

'Of course. I'm your husband.'

'I thought you were more than that. I thought you were my lover.'

'On our island, yes. Not here. Here you follow the rules set by my family. You have to be silent, Holly.'

'I don't believe,' she said softly, 'that silence was in the marriage vows.'

'You know it's why I married you.'

'Sorry?' She was past angry now, but she wasn't shouting. Maybe she even sounded reasonable. Softly enquiring of her husband what he meant.

'If the Calista royals had found you before we did…'

'Before…we?'

'My brother and I.'

'What would the royals of Calista have done?'

'They would have brought us down. Hell, Holly, I don't have to tell you this. I've never made a secret of it.'

'No,' she said, breaking eye contact to give her head a bit of space. She turned and stared out the car window. They were approaching the palace. Huge tree-lined avenues heralded the approach. They'd swept in the main gates but there was still half a mile to travel before they reached the main residence.

The gates had closed behind them. If she got out now…

'Look, Holly, I don't know how long Sebastian intends to keep you here…'

She gasped at that, swivelling back to stare at him again. 'Sebastian. *Sebastian!* So it's not up to us, how long our marriage lasts. It's not even up to you. It's up to Sebastian!'

'He's your future king.'

'Your future king,' she snapped.

'That's right,' he said. 'You can walk away.'

'When Sebastian says I can.'

'Yes.'

'It's got nothing to do with you?'

'Holly, this was never a real marriage. You know that. I have royal obligations and you…you can't even bear to shut up for one press call.'

'I can't, can I?'

'Holly…' He hesitated, then held out his hand to her in a gesture of entreaty. She stared down at it—a tanned, finely boned hand, complete with a wedding ring.

He was coaxing her to do the right thing. He'd done the right thing—by the nation. For the royal family. He'd married her in all honour. And then he'd bedded her in spectacular fashion—for why waste a perfectly good wife?

Only now the deed was done, normal life must resume. Stay in the background, shut up and wear beige. No, that was the rule she'd heard for the mother of the groom at weddings. Never for the bride.

But she wasn't a bride; at least not a royal one. Her husband was holding his hand out to her, commanding her to join with him, commanding her to keep up this pretence.

Fine. She would. But pretence it was. She ignored the hand, and grabbed Deefer who'd been sleeping on the seat beside her. She hugged him to her, holding him like a shield.

'I need to know how long,' she muttered.

'How long what?'

'Before I can go home,' she answered angrily.

'Holly, please…'

'Look, Andreas, let's agree. The whole situation is irrational. I hadn't figured it out until now, but finally I have. All right, Andreas, I'll stand back, shut up and wear beige. But you and Sebastian had better figure out a time frame to let me go, because wearing beige will make me crazy.'

* * *

It got worse. The servants were lined up to welcome them 'home'. It seemed Andreas had his own apartments in one wing of the vast Castle of Aristo. There were no less than fifteen uniformed servants lined up to receive them. Andreas walked down the line shaking hands, receiving congratulations. Holly followed, but the first time she tentatively went to shake a hand herself Andreas stopped her with a sharp little gesture of rebuke. The servant—a middle-aged woman—took a fast step back.

'This is Mme Pirentas, our housekeeper,' Andreas said, formally, and then proceeded to introduce each in turn. Valet, butler, footmen, housemaids, gardeners. Each made a formal bow to her, but she'd learned her lesson now and kept her hands to herself. And her tongue.

They'd just reached the end of the line when there was a stir inside the entrance. Two more liveried servants emerged, ushering out a woman between them. Queen Tia, Andreas's mother. The elderly queen walked down the steps, grasped Andreas's hands and kissed him on either cheek.

'My son,' she said softly, sounding worried. 'Welcome home. You are naughty to take your bride away when we needed you.'

'Three days, Mama,' Andreas said. 'Hardly an extended honeymoon.'

'No, but at such a time, with Alex still away... Sebastian has barely been able to contain himself.' Tia shook her head, her formal smile of welcome fading as she turned to Holly. 'Welcome home, my dear. I'll have someone show you to your apartments. Andreas, Sebastian is expecting you in your father's study. Now.'

'I should show Holly—'

'I'll organize Holly,' Tia said in a tone that reminded Holly forcibly of her son. Aristocratic. Determined. And sure that the Red Sea would part for her. 'You go. You're needed. Holly will understand, I'm sure.'

* * *

And that was that. Andreas disappeared. Holly was left with a dozen servants and the queen.

Holly will understand? No, she didn't. She should have felt lonely. Deserted and intimidated. Instead she was trying to control a fury that was threatening to overwhelm her.

'So I'll see my husband again…at dinner?' she asked and the queen flashed her an uncertain glance.

'I'm not sure. I believe Sebastian wishes him to travel to Greece.'

'Greece,' she said blankly. 'Um…with me?'

'You need to make yourself at home here.'

'Do I?'

'My dear…'

'Oh, you needn't worry,' Holly said, seeing dismay wash over the aristocratic features. 'I'm not about to make a scene. I've been told my role here is beige and that's what you'll get. So I'll stay here while my husband goes to Greece. When can I have an audience with Sebastian?'

'Pardon?

'It's Sebastian who pulls the strings round here, right? Then it's Sebastian who'll tell me when it's convenient for my marriage to end.'

'You mean His Majesty, Prince Sebastian,' Tia said severely. 'And I believe my son thinks it might be a good thing if it doesn't end.'

Holly's eyebrows did a hike skyward. 'Really?'

'It was a lovely performance in church.'

A performance. *A performance!*

'That's nice,' she said between clenched teeth. She bent down and picked up Deefer. She'd set him down to greet the servants but she had need of his small, plump presence. Her comfort dog.

'Give the dog to one of the men,' Tia said, looking uncertain. 'Is he yours?'

'Yes,' she said and her hold instinctively tightened.

'He can be looked after in the stables.'

'He'll stay with me.'

'My husband's rule is that we don't have animals in the palace.'

Her husband? Wasn't Aegeus dead?

Did the rules made by dead kings last for ever? And did the rules made by dead kings apply to her?

'That might create a problem,' Holly said cautiously. 'You're saying I have to sleep in the stables?'

Tia glanced nervously at the servants. They were out of hearing. Just. Her tone softened, becoming sympathetic. 'As a young bride I learned fast that I needed to obey the rules.'

Holly frowned. After how many years of marriage was Tia still obeying rules? 'But you're the queen now,' she said. 'The family matriarch. Surely you can make your own rules.'

'It's Sebastian who makes the rules now.'

'But he's your son.'

'This is hardly appropriate—'

'It's not, is it?' Holly said tightly. 'I'll discuss this with Andreas. Hopefully before he goes to Greece. Meanwhile have someone show me to my bedroom. With my dog. Or have someone show me to the stables. With my dog. Take your pick. Your call, Your Majesty.'

CHAPTER TEN

How had she ever said that? Stood up to the queen? Holly sat on the magnificent four-poster bed and tried to stop her teeth chattering. Deefer huddled in her arms and shook in sympathy.

'It was you,' she told him. 'You made me feel brave.'

She didn't feel brave. She felt small, insignificant and very alone.

'When do you think we'll see Andreas?' she whispered.

Deefer licked her face.

'Yeah, your kisses are great,' she told him. 'But they lack a certain finesse.'

She stirred restlessly, trying to quell the rising sense of fear and loneliness. How could she stay here alone? But if Andreas didn't intend staying here, was there a choice?

Maybe there was. But if she went home now it was the end. And she'd married for a reason. It was crazy to walk away now.

'And he'd probably haul me back in chains,' she whispered. 'I'm a captive wife, Deefer. I'll end up like Tia. Obedient and fearful after years of marriage.'

Another lick.

Unbidden her eyes filled. Dammit, she would not cry. She carried the little dog over to vast French windows opening to a balcony overlooking acres of manicured gardens.

A vision sprang to mind—dusty paddocks, gum trees, and a small white grave.

'You'll like it at Munwannay,' she told Deefer. 'And at least I'll have you with me this time.

'But I want it all,' she whispered to herself. 'I want you and Andreas and Munwannay. I want to be a family.'

'You're flying out at dawn. I have a list of contacts over there for you to work your way through.'

Andreas stared at his brother, his dark eyes clouded. 'I can't leave Holly here.'

'You can't take her with you. You need to move fast and move alone. You've trained in security—you're the only one with the skills and inside knowledge and discretion to do this. And you know what happens if the stone isn't found.'

'I don't give a damn about the stone.'

'Do you think I do?' Sebastian asked incredulously. 'But like me, you care about our country. You care about our people.'

'Zakari would make a decent ruler.'

'We don't know that,' Sebastian said ruthlessly. 'And there's too much at stake to take a chance. You don't have a choice.'

'I've never had a choice,' Andreas said grimly.

'Not when the livelihood of our people's at stake. No.'

'And when the stone's found?'

'Then you might find you like being a prince again,' Sebastian said, and allowed himself a glimmer of a smile. 'As I might relish the chance to be king. But meanwhile we do what we have to do, and we do it now. The security chief is here to brief you. Let's go.'

Two a.m. He opened the door with stealth as if he was wary she might be sleeping. Yeah, she might be sleeping if she wasn't so on edge every nerve ending felt frayed and exposed and standing on end.

He'd also forgotten one pup. Deefer was out of bed the minute the door opened, bounding across the bedroom, yelping in delight at seeing his long-lost friend.

Holly followed the examples of her nerves and sat bolt

upright. 'It's a bit early in our marriage to come creeping in after midnight,' she said scathingly. 'Wouldn't you say?'

'I had to—'

'Go to Greece. Your mother told me.'

'I'm not going until tomorrow.'

'Oh, goody.' She glanced at the clock on the gilt bedside table. 'But it is tomorrow. Do we have one day left before you go.'

'Holly, I'm sorry, but… Yes, it's today. I need to go early this morning.'

'You have to save the world. Your mother told me.'

'What else did she tell you?' he said, sounding apprehensive.

'That Deefer has to sleep in the stables.'

'I can see you took that one on board.' The pup was wriggling ecstatically round his legs, practically turning inside out. He hadn't had his beach run today. He was one bored dog. Andreas scooped him up, turned him over and started scratching his tummy.

'Don't start making up to my dog,' Holly snapped and Andreas smiled, walked across and sat on the bed. It was a very big bed. Huge. There was no reason Holly's heart should lurch just because Andreas had sat down.

Maintain the rage, she told herself breathlessly. It was the only defence she had in this situation and she surely needed a defence.

'Your mother says I need to have deportment lessons.'

'It'd be excellent if you would,' he said.

'Why would it be excellent?'

He put Deefer down onto the carpet, wriggled the fringe of the ancient Persian rug until Deefer was distracted and then left him to it. This conversation, it seemed, was more important than a mere priceless heirloom.

'Holly, maybe we could have a real marriage,' he said cautiously.

'A real marriage.' She repeated the words dumbly, trying to figure why she felt as if all her breath had been sucked out of her. Three little words. A real marriage.

'Our plan of a royal marriage has worked far better than we

dared hope. The people are seeing you as my Cinderella bride. You have enormous public sympathy. Sebastian thinks it could work.'

Sebastian. 'Does he just?' she retorted, fighting for equilibrium. 'I'll have you know—'

'And I want you.'

There it was again. Whoosh. The same gut feeling she'd felt at seventeen, the moment her father had introduced her. Multiplied by about a million.

'If you want me,' she said softly, almost to herself, 'then it's not about Sebastian. It's not about this country. It's about us.'

'That's right,' he said, and tugged the covers aside, pulled her up so she was hugged against him and softly kissed her. 'It's all about us.'

'But tomorrow…'

'I am a prince,' he said, almost sadly. 'I need to do what I need to do. I won't let this country be ruined. But for now… For now, my heart, there's only you.'

Until dawn, she thought, but it could only be a fleeting thought for Andreas was holding her, possessing her, demanding she respond and how could she help but respond?

He was right. There was only them.

Until dawn.

She woke and he was gone. She stirred in the too big bed, drowsy and sated with the after effects of loving. She turned sleepily to his side of the bed and it was empty.

Even Deefer wasn't with her. She looked over to the door and he was there, his little black nose pressed against the vast oak panelling. Andreas was gone, and Deefer had the air of a pup who'd be faithful for years.

'Come back to bed, Deef,' she whispered, but the pup just whined and put his nose hard against the crack at the base of the door. She flung back the covers and padded across to him, picked him up and carried him back. She slid back down under the covers and held him close.

A real marriage. Huh!

'You'll like Australia,' she whispered. 'You can be a real dog on the farm. And me… I can go back to being the real me.'

The lonely me. The me who mourns a dead baby and a lost love.

'Yeah, the Miss Haversham me,' she said, blinking and sitting bolt upright as she heard the echoes of what she'd just thought. 'Sitting alone for years in cobwebs and crumbling wedding cake.'

There was a knock on the door. A maid put her nose around, looking apologetic.

'If you please, ma'am,' she said. 'Her Majesty, Queen Tia, has scheduled your deportment lesson at ten. She says breakfast will be served for you in the grand dining room at eight, and an etiquette master will be on hand to show you through the protocols.'

She closed the door.

'Wow,' Holly whispered. 'Protocols, eh? We're having protocols instead of eggs and bacon?' She shivered. 'You know, Deef, I want to go home.'

But…

'I said I'd make a go of this marriage,' she said, addressing a spine that was starting to sag. 'Andreas says we need to be married and I believe him.'

But…

'But nothing,' she told herself. 'Don't even think about being homesick. Go bury yourself in…protocols.'

He was gone for eleven interminable days. Days when she wasn't permitted out of the castle gates.

'Everyone thinks you're still on honeymoon,' she was told by the bureaucrat who headed the public relations department for the royals. 'The public doesn't know Andreas has gone to Greece. Your honeymoon is a perfect front.'

A perfect front for a marriage. Sure. They were supposed to be on honeymoon, ensconced in their sumptuous apartments, gloriously in love. Andreas was in Greece. She was in…protocol hell?

'You will walk three steps behind your husband at all times. Watch his feet—the moment he pauses, you pause. If he turns back, if he attempts to speak to you, come up to within a step of him, listen, smile, make your response brief, never look as if you're disagreeing and then step back. Your husband is royal and you're not. He takes precedence in everything.'

'Yeah, but he's not here to take precedence,' she told Deefer on day eleven. She'd taken the little dog for a walk in the palace grounds—to the south because cameras could penetrate to the north and it was imperative she wasn't seen walking disconsolately alone. Even here she didn't feel at ease. There was music playing from the palace balconies. The princesses, she thought, wincing. She'd hardly seen them. They'd been too caught up with their own personal concerns to spend much time with her. And she didn't like their choice of music.

She didn't like this place.

'It'll be better when I get home,' Andreas had assured her in the brief phone calls he made. He'd sounded stressed and tired, which was the only reason she couldn't yell at him. Though eventually she'd yell. Quietly of course. In a very deferential manner. If he ever returned.

She'd been thinking for too long. She'd taken her eyes off her pup. She hauled herself to attention but it was too late. Deefer had headed off at a run towards the palace's ornamental lake.

Uh oh. Deefer had found the lake a week ago and there'd very nearly been trouble. Swans…

'Get back here,' she yelled in her best authoritative voice. But whether he heard her over the music or not, Deefer wasn't paying attention. He was bored. Holly had spent the morning in interminable lessons. The servants didn't like him wandering. They seemed to have almost a phobia about pets, instilled by the old king. He wasn't permitted anywhere Holly wasn't, so he'd been locked in her apartment.

Border collies were bred to work. It was in him, an innate

instinct to get out in the fields and round things up. And the only things here to round up were the palace swans, scattered on the far side of the ornamental lake, spread randomly over the grass as they searched for snails.

And now... Creatures randomly spread were an offence against nature for one highly bred collie. Deefer was round the lake in a blur of canine happiness, reaching the swans long before Holly could reach him; long before her yells had any impact.

He launched himself into their midst, yipping with high-pitched excitement, but working with the innate intelligence of his breed. After that first initial scattering he'd figured his mistake. Now he was racing round the outside of the entire group, causing them to rear up, flap their wings in alarm, back away, snapping, screeching...

A lesser pup than Deefer might be intimidated. These birds were three times his height. But a dog had to do what a dog had to do. He was darting in and out so fast the birds could hardly figure what he was doing. He had them totally bewildered. Amazingly they were even starting to cluster together. He was herding them like a professional. Why didn't they fly away? Holly thought, racing past the massed bushes between her and her dog.

And it was no longer just Holly who was panicking. There were shouts from the palace balconies, audible above the music. Others were running as well—the man Holly recognized as the head gardener and two younger men.

She glanced sideways at them as she ran—and then her heart seemed to freeze in her chest. One of the men had a gun. A rifle. He was raising it. Aiming...

'No,' she screamed. 'No.'

But the guy still had his gun levelled. He wasn't looking in her direction and the music was louder where he was. Could he hear her?

'No,' she screamed again. 'He's mine.' But the man was steadying. His companions had paused to give him freedom to aim.

She was so close. She rounded the last clump of bushes and launched herself in a flying tackle she didn't know she was capable of. But too late? Too late? The gun exploded in a blast of noise. She felt a sting across her cheek and heard a man's shouted expletive.

But she had him, Deefer, an armload of overexcited pup. She was lying full length, rolling with him under her, hugging him, weeping, while swans went everywhere. She didn't care, she didn't care, she had her pup. He was wriggling. He was okay. She closed her eyes...

'Holly...'

And amazingly, miraculously, she heard him. It was a shout from far away, but even so she heard the terror above the music.

Andreas.

Her face stung. She could feel the warm trickle of blood seeping down her cheek.

But Deefer was safe. He was wriggling frantically in her arms, desperate to escape, to continue his very important task.

'Holly!' The yell was nearer now, and someone switched the music off. She opened her eyes and rolled over, still holding her pup in her arms.

Facing men. All of them seemed to be groundsmen of some description. The guy with the rifle was staring down at her with horror. He was backing away, and by the look on his face he was expecting to be shot himself.

Then he was shoved aside, with such force that he almost fell. And Andreas was bending over her, his face such a picture of dread that she instinctively put her hand to her face in case his expression was right and the shot had been...dreadful.

It wasn't. She could feel a faint scoring of her skin and the blood was a mere trickle.

'It's just a scratch,' she said, more forcefully than she intended. Maybe she even sounded indignant, for the faces around her sagged in relief. But she only had the most fleeting of glimpses, for Andreas was bending over her, his fingers touching her face, his eyes searching for something more serious than the scratch on her cheek.

'My love,' he breathed, his voice cracking with raw fear, and he gathered her into his arms and tugged her hard against him. Somewhere in the middle Deefer, squashed, gave a muffled yelp of protest. But he was ignored.

Was she dreaming? She didn't care. Holly abandoned herself to the feel of Andreas holding her, to the feel of his shirt against her face. She'd be bleeding all over him and how much was the royal shirt worth? She didn't care. She stayed right where she was, unmoving, feeling his heartbeat, feeling his strength and his protection.

Her man had come home. When she most needed him, he was there.

It couldn't last. There were voices behind them, the men around them trying to explain, trying to justify. Finally Andreas put her back from him. Deefer stuck his nose out from between them, but both of them were holding him now. Andreas swung Holly and dog into his arms, then sank so he was sitting on the grass with his wife cradled against him, the little dog held in their four loving hands.

'Who shot my wife?'

It was a voice she'd never heard before. It held such anger, indescribable fury mixed with the remnants of fear, that Holly shivered. Andreas's hold on her tightened.

'Well?'

'If you please, sir…' It was the youngest of the grounds-men, the one with the gun. He took a step forward, and by the look on his face it was clear he was expecting the step to be his last.

'He was trying to shoot Deefer…' Holly managed, though her voice only managed a squeak. She looked up at the boy and thought he shouldn't be so afraid. Not when things were okay. Not when she had Andreas. 'I… At home we have to shoot wild dogs that get into the cattle.'

'That's it,' the boy said eagerly, and the eldest of the groundsmen nodded.

'That's right,' the man said. 'We've had five swans killed over the last year. Something's getting in through the boundary fences. The king's orders are to shoot to kill whatever it is that's killing them.'

'When my wife's in line of sight?' Andreas said incredulously. 'When you all know it's her dog?'

'I didn't know it was her dog. And she just came flying from nowhere,' the young man muttered, sounding sullen now. 'No princess can run like that. And she just threw herself at the dog...'

'If I hadn't you would have killed him,' Holly managed, defiant from the safety of Andreas's arms.

'Is she safe?'

The imperious demand from behind made them all start. A woman was making her way through the group of groundsmen and the men were falling back to let her past. It was Tia—of course it was. She was dressed in an immaculate linen suit and pearls that must be worth a king's ransom. Her heels were totally unsuitable for walking on the grass, but then would any shoe dare to sink if Tia was wearing it?

But she looked...frightened.

'She's safe, Mother,' Andreas said thickly and Tia's face showed instant relief. But only fleetingly. She had herself under control in an instant.

'I saw the dog attack the swans. You know your father's orders. These are his swans. He'll protect them at any cost.'

'At the cost of Holly's life?' Andreas demanded incredulously. 'I can't believe you'd think that.'

'Your father—'

'My father's dead,' Andreas said flatly. 'It's not what he thinks now. It's what you think.'

'Of course it's not what I think.' She turned to the groundsmen, dismissing them with a wave. 'Go back to work. I don't hold you responsible for the girl's hurt. You were following the king's orders.'

'But...' the young groundsman stammered, still dazed.

'My son's wife will recover,' Tia said. 'I can see from here it's a scratch.' She permitted herself a wintry smile. 'She'll hardly sue.' Then as the men hesitated she lowered her voice a notch. 'Leave. Now.'

They went. Leaving Andreas holding Holly and Deefer, and the queen looking down at them, her face impassive. With Andreas glaring back at his mother as if he couldn't believe what he was hearing.

'I don't understand why the swans didn't just fly away,' Holly muttered, searching for something—anything—to take the look of anger from the faces of both mother and son.

'They have their wings clipped,' Tia told her. 'They can't.'

'Despite the fact that swans will always come back to their home lake,' Andreas said softly, his voice still laced with fury. 'But my parents clip their wings to make sure.'

'Oh, for heaven's sake... These are your father's orders,' Tia said. Her voice wasn't as sure as it had been. She sounded suddenly shaky. 'You know that, Andreas. It's the way things are. And I told her to keep the dog in the stables.'

'Holly comes with a dog. This is Holly's home, Mother.'

'It's not my home,' Holly said, struggling in his arms. He released her, reluctantly. She pushed herself to her feet and Andreas followed. She was feeling a little bit sick, she discovered. Her legs weren't as steady as she wanted them to be. She needed to pull away from both of these royals—she needed to face them square on—but she needed Andreas's support. But she still knew what needed to be said. 'My home's in Australia and I'm leaving.'

'You can't leave yet,' Tia said, shocked, as Andreas's expression snapped into a frown, and Holly shook her head.

'I can leave any time I want. Isn't that so, Andreas?'

He tugged her tight against him. She could feel the tension in his body; she could feel how close he was to snapping. There were tensions here that didn't have anything to do with her. There were tensions she didn't understand.

'That's right,' he said softly, but there was no mistaking the steel behind the quiet words as he met his mother's gaze, unflinching. 'Holly married me to get us out of a mess. She's fulfilled her part of the bargain. We've told the press that she'll keep her property back in Australia, with intermittent visits from me. She's free to go.'

'Sebastian thinks it will be better if she stays,' Tia said sharply.

'Sebastian does not rule my private life,' Andreas snapped. 'As my father no longer rules yours. Maybe we both have to learn that. Meanwhile my wife is my business. If I say she can go, then she can go.'

'Thanks very much,' Holly managed and would have wrenched away but he was still holding her hard against him. Her face was still bleeding. A droplet splashed on the white cotton of her shirt. She put her fingers up to her cheek and he noticed.

'I need to get you inside and have that seen to,' he said ruefully.

'She *will* stay,' Tia said in a voice that sounded almost desperate.

'How are you going to clip my wings?' Holly said shakily. Shock was setting in for real now. Deefer was limp in her arms as if the little dog also realized just how close they'd come to calamity. 'I'm free,' Holly said, forcing herself to continue. 'Andreas... Andreas is my husband but that's not enough to hold me. I'm going home.'

Ignoring her protests, he carried her out through the palace kitchens to a room that was set up as a first-aid centre. The vast palace staff would make a first-aid centre essential, Holly thought, though she wasn't up to thinking much. She lay back in Andreas's arms, she hugged Deefer and she let him take her where he willed. She might have sounded defiant before Tia, but inside she was a wimpering wreck.

'Wh...when did you get back?' she managed as he shoved open the clinic door with his foot and carried her inside.

'Ten minutes ago. I came to find you straight away.'

'You could have come earlier,' she whispered and then thought if he'd come even a couple of minutes earlier she might have been distracted enough not to notice what Deefer was doing until too late. She shivered involuntarily and his hold on her tightened.

'Hell, Holly, I thought you'd be safe.'

'Yeah, well, you will have thugs with guns.'

'They're not my thugs.'

'No, but they're hired by your family. And you're a part of this family, Andreas.'

'I am,' he said grimly, and then a buxom, motherly woman hustled into the room, all starch and cluck, and they couldn't talk for she took over their talking for them.

It was as Holly had thought—a long scratch, only bleeding in the middle. The bullet had barely grazed the surface. But the nurse examined it from all angles, then discussed with Andreas whether it was worth calling in the royal physician. 'No,' Holly said hotly, but she was ignored, though their conclusion was the same. But the wound was cleaned and dressed with all the care in the world.

At the end of her ministrations Holly was left with a face that any self-respecting bacterium would find blocked from twenty paces, and a huge white dressing that would have done a lobotomy proud.

'You know, when I'm rounding up cattle I get plenty of scratches as bad as this,' she said as finally the nurse released them from her clutches and they left the room. 'From overhead branches. They sure don't get dressed like this.'

'They should,' Andreas growled.

'You're suggesting I install a first-aid clinic at Munwannay with your money?'

'If you want one, you can have one.'

'I don't want one,' she said, revolted. They were walking slowly back to their apartment. Andreas was holding Deefer tucked under one arm. With his other hand he was holding Holly's. She should pull back, she thought. This was such a temporary marriage. But he was holding her as if he loved her.

She'd go home soon, she thought drearily. This morning's events had cemented that for her. But she'd remember this. Two brief snatches of time with the man she'd love for ever. One time ten years ago. And now... Her hand tightened convulsively and he looked down at her and smiled.

'You missed me?'

'That's an unfair question.' She swallowed, not wanting to ask but knowing she needed to. 'Will you be staying? Or...do you need to go away again?'

'I do,' he said seriously. 'Tomorrow.'

'For how long?' she whispered, her heart sinking.

'I don't know.'

'I can't stay here...without you.'

'I understand that,' he said, and the hint of a smile disappeared from his face. 'I hoped...but today, yes, it's clear. Deefer is a dog bred to be a working dog. You're bred to be free. I will not let my mother clip your wings.'

'She couldn't.'

'She could try. This whole damned household will try. My mother is a good woman but she's been ruled by my father for too long to escape the royal protocol.'

'You wouldn't...' She hesitated but it had to be said. It had to be asked. Pride or not, this was her man and she had to fight for him if she could. 'You would never consider...coming to Australia?'

'I will visit,' he said.

Visit. Of course. Once a year?

'Of course,' she said flatly. 'To keep up the pretence of our marriage.' And then because she couldn't help herself she added... 'How often?'

'I don't know,' he said honestly. They were in their apartment now. He led her over to the bed and they sat side by side. He set Deefer onto the floor but the little dog was subdued. He knew things were grim. He huddled in against Holly's legs and stayed.

'I can't do as I want, Holly,' he said. 'I was born into this job.'

'And your country needs you.'

'It does,' he said simply. 'Whether it knows it or not.'

'I... That's okay,' she said and swallowed. 'I didn't really expect you to come back with me.'

'I'll come as often as I can.'

'You know, maybe it'd be better if you didn't,' she said miserably. 'You were gone for years and I couldn't forget you. If you keep popping back every six months or so...'

'I'll come more often than that.' He turned her face to his and kissed her on the nose. 'You are my wife.'

'In name.'

'In law,' he said strongly. 'I want you, Holly. I want you here, in my bed, but I accept that's not possible. My father clipped the wings of his wild creatures. I will not.'

'Andreas—'

'Hush,' he said and gathered her to him. 'Just hush, my love. Yes, I have to leave again tomorrow, and I'll arrange for you to leave as well. I'll organize a boat to take you to Greece. I have friends there who'll see you cared for; who'll organize your forward journey to Australia. The press will be told there are urgent matters you need to attend to in Australia. There's no need to fear Sebastian will haul you back. The scandal would be worse than if we'd never married.'

He had it all planned, she thought numbly. She should protest. But all she could do was listen.

'Money's already been transferred to your working account,' he was saying. 'You'll find the mortgages on Munwannay have been cleared. There's a lump sum for restocking and money for staffing. You're to get good staff, mind, Holly. You're to have skilled help or I'll know the reason why. By the time I visit, I expect to see the Munwannay I first saw—a vibrant, working farm. A family home.'

'I—'

'You can do this, Holly,' he said strongly, not letting her interject. 'It's what you've always wanted. And there will be no long-term problem here. Our people understand royal marriages. They think it's wonderful to have an Australian princess, but they know my royal duties have to take precedence. It will be accepted.'

'But Sebastian—'

'This has nothing to do with Sebastian now.'

'Or your mother?'

'No. But I owe them a duty of care—that's why I need to keep looking for the diamond.'

'And you owe me…'

'What I owe you I've paid in full.'

'Have you, Andreas?' She swallowed hard, trying not to cry. 'Have you? Oh, you've married me in all honour. You've given me the Cinderella story. Now you've paid for my happy ever after. I should be grateful. But…' She swallowed, fighting for words. 'I want more,' she managed, but she looked into his eyes and knew he didn't understand.

'Holly, this was a business arrangement,' he said softly. 'A marriage of necessity. I'm sorry it can't be more.'

'Well, so am I,' she snapped, suddenly furious. 'Business arrangement? No way. Not on my part. I made my vows and I meant them.'

'Yet you don't wish to stay.'

She stared at him, baffled. He didn't get it. Was it only she who was hungry for what was just in front of them, so close but yet so far? She ached for him to hold her in his arms, to tell her she was indeed his wife, that he'd never let her go. Instead he talked of his duty of care to his family.

'I think you should go now,' she whispered.

'Go…'

'Back to wherever you've been diamond hunting. Or wherever.'

'I don't leave until the morning. I'd hoped—'

'Well hope away, Your Highness,' she snapped. 'I've just had a very nasty shock. I've been shot at and I'm wounded. I have a headache and if you think I'm going to bed with you when I have a headache…'

'The Holly I knew would never let a headache stop her.'

'Yeah, well, the Holly you knew was a dope,' she whispered. 'The Holly you knew has gone far enough in this royal charade and can go no further. Enough, Andreas. Leave please.'

'Holly…' He caught her hands and drew her round, forcing her to face him. 'I can't believe you mean that.' He smiled, that fabulous, gentle, seductive smile that made her toes curl, that was the source of all the trouble in the first place. 'You don't want me?'

'I can't want you,' she said miserably. 'Can't you see that? Please, Andreas, no more. To be kind…just leave.'

What had she done? He stared at her for a long, tension-filled moment, his face expressionless. Then, without another word, he stood up and walked out of the room, closing the door behind him. She was left staring after him in dismay.

She'd sent him away.

He was leaving anyway in the morning.

But she wanted this night.

It wasn't going to make anything better, she thought drearily. She'd thought she could take as much of Andreas as he offered, but all his nearness did was make her ache for more.

He'd gone. She didn't have to see him again. She could stay in her room for the rest of the day, plead headache, sleep, then when she woke he'd have left.

A stronger woman would fight for him.

Was it strong to stay in this place? Submit to endless protocol, endless absences, the clipping of her wings?

'I'd be a bird in a gilded cage,' she whispered to Deefer, hugging him close. 'I can't. Even for Andreas.'

Yet to leave him…

I'm not leaving him. He's doing the leaving.

If you walked to the door now and called him back he'd come. Until dawn.

'Oh, Deef.' She was crying, stupid helpless tears slipping down her cheeks, one after another. She hated crying. She never cried.

Andreas made her cry.

'Which is as good a reason as any to leave,' she told her dog. 'I have to go. I must.'

It'd break her heart.

No. Her heart had broken years ago and the pieces were still apart. For a few short days the pieces had made a tentative effort to heal. But it hadn't worked. Of course it hadn't. Cinderella was for fairy tales.

She had to go…home.

He walked outside, into the palace forecourt. The sun was blazing down on the marble columns, the shining granite steps radiating heat. The white pebbles of the paved surfaces shimmered in the sun, and the vast ornate fountain gave no sense of relief. This was formality at its finest. Formality at its worst.

He lived here. It was his life.

He thought of where Holly was heading—to a vast outback wilderness, a place where nature couldn't help but win over any attempt to tame it, and a wave of longing swept over him so strongly that it felt as if he had to physically brace himself against its force.

Munwannay and Holly.

Holly.

He couldn't keep her here. Her place was in Munwannay. How he'd ever thought he could hold her this long…

He'd brought her here against her will and he would not keep her. Despite Sebastian. Despite his mother. They were wrong. Holly was wild and beautiful and free and he would not tame her.

His fingers were clenched so hard into his palms that they hurt. He stared down and saw he'd pierced the skin on one palm. It hurt, but compared to the gut-wrenching pain inside it was nothing. To let her go…

He had to let her go.

There was a stir behind him. He turned to find two servants pushing the door wide, and Sebastian striding out towards him.

'I told you I wanted to see you the minute you arrived,' he snapped.

'Holly needed me.'

'I have no interest in what Holly needs. You know this matter's urgent. I want your report and I want it now. For me to have to come and find you…'

'Unforgivable,' Andreas said dryly. 'You want my head off at dawn?'

'Don't be facetious. You know how much is at stake. I need you to be focused.'

'Of course.'

Sebastian's eyes narrowed. 'I mean it, Andreas.'

'Of course you do,' Andreas said wearily. 'And, yes, I know how urgent it is. Yes, I know how much our country is depending on me staying focused. It'll happen. Holly's leaving tomorrow for Australia.'

'What?' Sebastian snapped, his features darkening in displeasure. 'I told you, I wanted the marriage to last.'

'And I'm telling you the marriage is over,' Andreas replied, and his voice sounded strong and sure, two emotions that were surely as far from the truth as it was possible to get. 'Short of locking us in a dungeon there's nothing you can do about it, brother. So set your public relations department to make as good a job of it as they can, but the thing's not negotiable. Holly goes home tomorrow. End of story.'

CHAPTER ELEVEN

IT WAS amazing. First there was a journey to Greece on a fishing boat with friends of Andreas. That was the part of the trip where Sebastian could have intervened, she was told, so she had to stay with men Andreas trusted. Then she and Deefer were whisked to the airport. What followed was first-class air travel, with personal attention all the way. Before she knew it, she landed in Perth where she bade a tearful farewell to Deef. Her pup had to face thirty days in quarantine before he could become an Australian. As she came out of the customs building she was met by a pilot upset that she'd got this far without him finding her. It seemed a private helicopter had already been chartered to take her on to Munwannay.

Her financial circumstances only a month ago might have seen her hitch-hiking. This was a turnaround indeed.

She should feel flattered and indulged. Instead she felt miserable.

And as soon as they arrived at Munwannay she saw more signs of change. From the air she could see people moving about, a couple of shiny new vehicles, two men on horseback.

It seemed that Andreas's promised money had reached Munwannay before she had.

They landed and a lean, weathered man in his late fifties came striding across the dusty paddock to greet her. There was a rangy blue-heeler at his side. A dog, back on Munwannay.

'Afternoon, ma'am,' he said with a slow, lazy smile that told her more than anything else that he'd been bred in the bush. 'I'm Bluey Crammond.' He motioned to the dog. 'This here's Rocket. Your husband's sent me here to help set the place up as it ought to be set up. If you and Rocket and I get on, your husband's thinking I could stay on as your overseer, but that's up to you. Rocket and I are here on three months' probation— if you think we're suitable and I think the place is a goer then we'll stay. But I'm telling you now, this place is fantastic. Your husband says you have ideas and I'm just waiting to hear them.'

He smiled, a slow, farmer's grin. Rocket extended a paw on command and Holly was smitten.

As she was with the housekeeper waiting for her in the homestead. Margaret Honeywell was a lovely, plump lady who reminded Holly forcibly of Sophia.

'Your husband says I'm here for a trial period only, and if you find the idea of staff intrusive then I'll go,' she told her. 'Bluey and I have been paid well to come here for the trial period, so you're not to think we'll mind if you let us go. But I'm hoping you won't.'

Holly was already sure that she wouldn't. Somehow Andreas had picked staff whose credentials—and personalities—were wonderful.

He must have started organizing almost before they were married, she thought, dazed, for Bluey and Mrs Honeywell— 'call me Honey, love, everyone else does'—had been employed through an agency in Perth and had been at Munwannay for a week before she'd arrived.

Their work was stunning. The homestead was gleaming under Honey's industrious enthusiasm. Fencing contractors had been hired, repairing the ravages of years of neglect. Outbuildings were being repaired. Skilled mechanics were checking bores, repairing and replacing machinery that was well past its use-by date and making sure there was water for cattle that could be bought any time she said the word.

'I'm happy to come to the market with you,' Bluey told her

deferentially. 'But His Highness says you know cattle better'n anyone in the country and I'm not wanting to step on your toes. And he said you had the funds for a great herd.'

She did. When she checked her bank account she couldn't believe the figures. She had enough and more to get this place back to what it should be.

She should be deliriously happy. To have enough money to restore Munwannay to its former glory was a dream come true. But...

But for a start she didn't have Deefer. As a pup bred for possible international sale, Deefer had been given all the appropriate vaccinations from the breeder so he could travel anywhere, but still he had to endure his four weeks' quarantine. Rocket was great but he wasn't Deefer.

And of course the biggie.

She didn't have Andreas.

And that was a stupid thing to be pining for, she thought savagely as the days wore on. If she hadn't left then she'd be pining for Andreas back at Aristo, while she endured stupid lessons in decorum. At least here she could get her hands dirty. She could go wherever she wanted.

For out in the stables she found another example of her husband's organization. Whippy, grandson of Merryweather. Merry had died two years back of old age, a note from Andreas had told her, but his investigators had found her Whippy—who looked and worked so like his grandmother it was love at first sight.

So now she could ride as she loved to ride. She could work side by side with Bluey, pushing herself so hard she fell into her bed at night physically spent. She could make plans for her cattle station. She could go back to teaching if she wanted.

She could start her life again.

So she shouldn't lie awake night after night thinking of Andreas. Thinking if she'd stayed at the palace then maybe every couple of weeks he'd have come to her bed. Thinking maybe that could have been enough.

Thinking she was mad to come home.

When Deefer came it'd be better, she told herself desperately, but she knew it wouldn't be. She'd ached for Andreas for years and these last weeks had turned that ache into a piercing physical pain.

A week after she arrived he telephoned. She'd just walked in after an afternoon riding Whippy round the northern reaches of the property, checking her magnificent new bores and talking fencing with Bluey. She was hot, dusty and exhausted. She walked up the steps of the veranda, and Honey was holding out the phone and beaming.

'It's your husband.'

Your husband. Honey was smiling as if this was completely normal. Her husband was phoning from where he lived to where she lived.

It felt…wrong.

It was a sham marriage, but if it was sham then surely she shouldn't think of him as her husband. Surely no one should refer to him as her husband.

'H…hi,' she managed, and there was silence on the end of the phone for so long she thought the connection must have died.

'Hi, yourself,' he said at last. He sounded tired and strained. 'How are things?'

'Good. I mean…great.' She fought for composure. 'I can't believe you found Whippy.'

'I wished I could have found Merry,' he said softly. 'I loved her, too.'

By the sound of his voice she knew he spoke nothing but the truth. She swallowed, thinking of the young Andreas, riding side by side with her all those years ago, loving this place, loving this work. If he could only come…

No. He was royal. Husband in name only.

'The people you employed are fantastic, too,' she managed. 'I don't know how you found them.'

'I'm good at finding fantastic people,' he growled. 'Or…a fantastic person. One wife, for instance.'

162   THE PRINCE'S CAPTIVE WIFE

'Don't,' she whispered. She shook herself, trying to get rid of the wash of unreality. He was half a world away. No. He was of another world.

'Andreas, this money... There's so much.'

'I hope it's enough,' he said, 'to tide you over until the place is self-supporting. Bluey says you should be able to do it, but ask if you need more.'

'You can't give me this.'

'You're the mother of my son,' he growled. 'I love Munwannay as much as you do and I want it restored. I can give you what I damned well want, and you'll take it.'

'Ooh, the arrogance,' she said before she could stop herself, and there was a pause. When he spoke again the tension had eased a little. She could hear a smile in his voice.

'As disrespectful as ever, then?'

'Who, me?'

'Yes, you,' he said and she knew he was smiling. 'My outback girl. My Cinderella princess.'

'I'm not your anything, Andreas,' she said softly and she heard the smile disappear.

'No.'

'You're home in Aristo?'

'Briefly.'

'You're still diamond hunting?'

There was a sharp intake of breath. 'Holly, that stays with you. If it got out—'

'I'm talking to you—on this phone line you've organized that's encrypted. Honestly, Andreas—'

'It's necessary,' he snapped. 'If you're going to be indiscreet—'

'I have an encrypted phone. I can be as indiscreet as I want.'

'Holly...'

'Yes?' She sounded angry, she thought, but she couldn't stop herself. This was crazy. A prince calling her his Cinderella princess. Encrypted phones. Money to spare.

'Are you happy?'

The question caught her off guard. 'Of course I'm not happy,' she snapped before she could stop herself.

'Why not?'

Because I love you, you big oaf, she thought, but she couldn't say it. 'I'm missing Deefer,' she said at last.

'When can you get him?'

'Three weeks. I need to collect him at the quarantine station in Perth.' She swallowed. 'We have cattle arriving on the same day he's due for release. He'll have to wait an extra twenty-four hours until I can fetch him. I know it's crazy but I got upset when I found out.'

'Pay someone to collect him for you.'

'I'll collect him myself,' she said, trying really hard not to sound choked up. 'I… Was there anything else you wanted?'

'Can I talk to Bluey?'

'Checking up on me?'

'Yes,' he said strongly. 'Yes, I am. I worry about you, Holly. I've heard you're working too hard.'

'And so are you,' she snapped. 'I can hear in your voice that you're exhausted, but I can't ring your henchmen and ask for reports.'

'I'm not—'

'How much sleep did you get last night?'

'That's none of—'

'My business,' she finished for him. 'No. For I'm not your wife, Andreas. As you're not my husband. Let's leave the checking alone. Let's leave each other alone. Thank you so much for what you've done for the farm,' she said stiffly, forcing herself to say what had to be said. 'But if there's nothing else… Thank you for calling and goodbye.'

He replaced the receiver and stood, staring at the phone for a long time. Sebastian, searching for him on business, found him still standing at his desk, and at the look on his face he frowned in swift concern.

'What is it? Problems? The diamond…'

'No problem.' He shook his head, trying to clear his mind of the emotion caused by the call. 'Not as far as I know. I'm leaving for Spain in the morning. We're working through every avenue.'

'I know you're doing what you can,' Sebastian growled and, uncharacteristically, he put his hand on his brother's shoulder. 'You're looking like hell, brother.'

'I've just sent my wife to Australia.'

'Not my idea,' Sebastian said firmly. 'In fact, I seem to remember I forbade it. There are repercussions already. The people don't like you parting so soon, no matter how sensibly you've explained it.'

'So tell me I can go to her.'

'Bring her back here,' Sebastian said. 'You're needed here. These next few weeks are vital to secure the country.'

'And after that?'

'You're third in line to the throne. You know your place is here. We're family, brother, whether you like it or not, and you know your duty.'

'So it's Spain tomorrow. While Alex honeymoons.'

'He'll be back. He knows his place.'

'And he even enjoys it.'

'Enjoyment doesn't come into it. Family does.'

'Right.'

'You're not thinking—'

'Of course I'm thinking,' Andreas snapped, shrugging off his brother's hand. 'I'm thinking so hard my head hurts. I need to get some rest.' He paused and a glimmer of a smile returned behind his eyes. 'Even my wife says I'm tired. My wife.'

'It's a marriage of convenience.'

'Yes,' he said and closed his eyes. 'A marriage of convenience. Family… Hell, Sebastian, let me be. Spain tomorrow. Duty calls.'

She bathed away the dust of the day, she picked at the truly excellent dinner Honey put before her, and then she wandered down through the home paddock to the Munwannay gum tree.

To sink on the grass round her little son's grave. To close her eyes and let pain wash over her in waves so great she thought they'd overwhelm her.

'I can do this,' she whispered. 'I can go on.'

For whom?

'There's no choice,' she told the little boy buried deep under the leaf litter. 'I love Munwannay. It's my home.'

'Your home's with your husband,' she told herself.

'He doesn't need me.' She knew that. 'He even agreed I should be here.'

'It'll be better when Deefer's here,' she whispered but no one answered. No one agreed.

Her little son was gone. Her husband was in another world.

She was alone.

The first of the cattle arrived the day Deefer's quarantine expired. There was nothing Holly wanted more than to fly down to Perth and fetch him, but these cattle were the beasts she'd chosen herself.

Bluey was good but he'd stayed at Munwannay while she'd attended the sales so he didn't know what she was expecting. Cattle had been switched before. She had to be here when they arrived, to check they were the beasts she'd bought, to welcome the beginning of Munwannay's rebirth as a prosperous cattle station.

They started arriving at dawn, in a string of road-trains, huge trucks loaded with bewildered beasts. Every truck had to be checked, cattle ticked off individually as they were unloaded, trucks directed to individual paddocks. The cattle would be held in the near paddocks and hand-fed until they settled, then gradually assimilated into a life of freedom, roaming the vast open landscape around them. These were magnificent breeding stock. She'd got it right, Holly thought in satisfaction as she worked on. It'd be okay. She could do this.

And if she worked really hard she might be able to put Andreas out of her mind.

She worked on all through the day, ceaselessly checking cattle, giving orders, working side by side with Bluey and the two other men they now employed. They needed more staff yet, she thought. A couple of jillaroos or jackaroos. They needed more cattle, too.

And tomorrow she'd fly to Perth to collect Deefer. That should make her the happiest of women. She had nothing left to complain about.

So why did she feel so empty?

At seven that night she saw the last of the trucks drive off the property. Even Bluey was beat. He headed back to his quarters with Rocket beside him and Holly watched them go and thought wistfully that tomorrow she'd have her own dog.

Honey had set up a trestle table of food out under the gums. Holly and the men had eaten intermittently during the day, grabbing sandwiches in passing. Honey was there now, clearing away. She glanced up at Holly, who was standing on the veranda looking into middle distance.

'You want something else to eat, love?'

'No, thanks. I might just have a bath and hit the cot.'

'You might want to rethink that,' Honey said and glanced at her watch. 'You're expecting a visitor.' She shaded her eyes and stared up into the western sky. 'Speaking of the devil…' She smiled. 'Right on cue.'

'Who…?'

'He rang before,' Honey said. 'When you were down the bottom paddock. He reckoned he'd be here at seven. "Make sure she's home," he told me, and where else would you be? I asked him. So here he is. Do you reckon he'll need a sandwich?'

'I…who?'

'Who do you think?' Honey said and beamed and collected a pile of plates and walked up the veranda steps. 'Who do you think, indeed?' she repeated as she walked past Holly and through the door into the kitchen. 'Some wife you make.'

For it was him. Of course it was him. The chopper settled

in the same dusty paddock it had landed that first day, carrying
Sebastian's thugs. Georgiou stepped out first and for one awful
moment Holly expected the other three men to follow.

But she needn't have worried. Georgiou hauled open the
door to the rear, and it was Andreas who stepped lightly out
onto the dust and looked up to the house.

Andreas. And in his arms…

Deefer.

'Deefer,' Holly whispered as if it were the little dog who
mattered most and not the man holding him.

'Call him,' Andreas yelled as the sound of the motor died to
nothing. Holly was already moving numbly down the veranda
steps, her legs operating without any conscious thought.

'Deefer,' she called as if in a dream, and Andreas set the little
dog down and he barrelled across the paddock so fast he was
a black and white blur. He didn't check until he reached her.
She stooped a little but not much—she didn't need to—for he
was leaping high, with one bound flying straight into her arms.
His rough little tongue was licking her from chin to forehead
and his whole body was wriggling in ecstasy.

'Deefer. Oh, Deef,' Holly said and would have burst into
tears. But there was no room for tears for Andreas was striding
across the gap between them, almost as fast as Deefer. Before
she knew it she was gathered into his arms, held in a grip of
iron with Deef somehow sandwiched in between.

'What…? What…?'

'You said you couldn't collect Deefer yourself,' he said,
and smiled down at her with a look of such tenderness that
something melted deep inside. That he look at her like this…

It'd only be a flying visit. She had to get hold of herself. She
couldn't afford to melt.

She couldn't.

'You planned this.'

'I hoped it'd work out. I couldn't promise, because I've just
come back from France.'

So it was a flying visit. A reassurance to his people that there was a marriage. She could barely make herself speak. How could she bear it? That he come and go again at will?

'How…how long are you staying?' she whispered and she could barely get the words out. Her face was muffled against his chest and a fair bit of Deefer was interfering with her ability to speak as well.

He laughed and set her back from him. His black eyes gleamed, with laughter and with something else. Something she'd never seen before.

Assurance? Strength? He truly was a royal prince, she thought. Until this moment she'd never thought of him as truly royal—he'd just been her Andreas who she loved with all her heart. But there was that about him now that spoke of absolute assurance. As if his entire lineage of royal ancestry was right behind him, making him who he was.

'I'm staying for as long as you want me,' he told her and her heart stilled within her chest.

'As long…'

'As long as you'll have me, my heart,' he told her and he bent and kissed her with such tenderness that she could scarcely bear it.

She must have misheard. There must be some sort of catch. But she wasn't releasing him. He was kissing her and she was kissing him back with such fierce possessiveness that surely he couldn't let her go.

But finally he did, setting her back, holding her shoulders in his hands and smiling down into her eyes.

'I suspect Deefer needs air.'

In Holly's arms Deefer wriggled with grateful comprehension. Andreas smiled and set the little dog down.

Rocket was out near the overseer's quarters, wandering over to investigate these newcomers. Deefer saw him from the distance, wriggled in ecstasy and launched himself forward into his new life.

'Will he be okay?' Andreas asked.

'Rocket's a great dog,' Holly managed, turning slightly

within the crook of Andreas's arm. As if to confirm it, the big, old dog crouched low, then rolled over before the puppy reached him, in an attitude of complete subjection.

'Is that healthy?' Andreas demanded.

'Probably not.'

'Training tomorrow, then,' Andreas said. 'Deference to your elders, lesson one.'

'You will be here tomorrow?'

'Yes.' He kissed her.

She allowed him to kiss her. When she'd been kissed to her satisfaction—for now—she pushed back a little. Deefer was jumping over and over Rocket in the dust. Bluey had come out his back door and was watching…the dogs. Honey had the curtains of the front room twitched aside and was watching…the dogs.

'We have an audience,' Holly murmured, and giggled.

'Then we should put on a show,' Andreas said and tugged her to him.

She took a deep breath, forcing her knees to steady and her voice to sound a little resolute. As resolute as she could manage. 'Explain.'

'Explain what?'

'How you can just calmly walk back into my life.'

'I'm saving my country,' he said, sounding virtuous. 'As a noble prince who knows his duty to his people, I can do nothing else.'

'You've a kangaroo loose in the top paddock.'

He looked wounded. He set her back again and held her at arm's length. 'You're saying I'm crazy? Me, who brought you your dog.'

'Virtue all round. Bringing me my dog. Saving your country. Would you mind telling me how?'

'Easy,' he said, and he smiled and it was the smile that Holly loved and it was almost enough for her to say forget the explanations, just head straight to the bedroom, because it had been a really long month and that smile made her toes curl. But somehow she forced herself to be patient. Somehow she let him keep smiling at her while he had his say.

'You were a hit,' he said. 'The people of Aristo love you. Or they love what they saw of you. There was a public outcry when you left.'

'I don't believe you.'

His smile faded. 'You need to believe me,' he said softly, 'because it's true. I've had to be away so much we put out rumours that I'd come home with you. Only then your local press investigated and found I wasn't here.'

'They phoned,' Holly said, dismayed. 'What was I supposed to do? Lie?'

'I didn't ask you to lie,' he said. 'I'd never expect it of you. So then Sebastian said you need to come back to Aristo.'

She sighed. 'For a spot of wing clipping?'

'That's what I said,' he told her, starting to smile again. 'And I can't see you with clipped wings.'

'So…'

'So there's general unrest that our marriage was just for show. The people like you. The royal PR department has been putting it about that we have a Cinderella marriage. Sebastian's been talking at me about putting my family first. And it suddenly occurred to me…'

'What?' she said, sounding suddenly breathless. Feeling suddenly that there was a chink in a very heavy door and light was filtering through. Just maybe…maybe…

'That you are my family,' he said and the smile was back for real now, tender, warm and loving. 'I hadn't seen it until then, but suddenly there it was. You, Holly, are my wife. You live here, a place I love and where I want to work. My son is buried here. My dog was waiting for someone to collect him to bring him home. And if our people want the Cinderella story, then what better than you choosing your prince and rescuing him, carrying him to his happy ever after? Here.'

She could scarcely breathe. She was staring at him as if he'd grown two heads. 'You…you'd leave Aristo for me?'

'I have,' he said softly. Then, at the look on her face, he shook his head. 'No. I haven't run from my duty. The corruption commission has come to an end. I've done all the searching I can for the diamond, and, no, don't ask me whether it's been found because I can't and won't tell you. It's irrelevant to us now.'

'But…your mother. Sebastian…'

'They were my family,' he said gently. 'After my father's harsh rule they need to reassess what's important to them as well, and maybe they are. My mother is taking the first few tentative steps right now. But for me… For me the path is clear. I have a new family. I have a wife and a dog and a vast cattle property in Australia. I have a fabulous island getaway off Aristo that we can still use for holidays. I have you.'

'But you can't,' she said, dazed. 'You're third in line to the throne.'

'No more,' he said and he tugged her to him and held her tight. 'I made that very clear when I addressed the people of Aristo on national television two nights ago. My brother's perfectly capable of running the country. He has Alex at his side. Plus—and this is the big plus, Holly—he also has my sisters. Sebastian hasn't seen it until now. Like me, he was brought up to believe women were to be relegated to the background, but I know he's wrong. I told him so. I've told my mother and my sisters and I've told my country. I've done all I'm capable of to make my country safe, and now it's me time. Us time,' he corrected himself. 'If that's okay with you, my love. You have a pretty big place here. Do you think we could share?'

She gasped on a sob. She was holding him tight, her hands on his hips, not letting him move from her grasp, but she was watching his face as if it might disappear at any minute. As if truth could turn to falsehood. But what she saw there was only truth.

Her husband. Her love.

Did he think they could share? She turned to stare around her, at the endless plains where the cattle were just starting their first tentative exploration. As she was about to start tentatively exploring the realities of a marriage.

'I think we might just find room,' she whispered. 'If you truly mean it.'

'How can I not mean it?' He gave a whoop of triumph, lifted her high and brought her down to kiss her. 'My love. My Cinderella wife.'

'My Cinderella husband,' she said. And then she had a thought. 'Um…does this mean I'm not a princess any more?'

'Inherited title,' he said, sounding smug. 'Ancient lineage. Titles can't be removed by mere abdication. You're still a princess.'

'They won't call you prince round here. You'll get called Rass, like you got from the men when you worked with them years ago.'

'Rass sounds great to me.'

'Then R… Rass?'

'Yes, my love?'

'Do you suppose we could go inside?' she whispered. 'Everyone's watching.'

'And what would you like to do that you can't do while everyone's watching?'

'Come inside and find out.'

It was almost two in the morning when she stirred. This had happened these last few nights, the vague feeling in the small hours that things were not quite right.

How could they not be right tonight? She was coiled in her husband's arms, tucked tight against him, skin against skin, naked, exposed, as one with the man she loved.

This was where she wanted to be for the rest of her life. She knew it with the same certainty as she believed Andreas. He'd said it last night in the aftermath of lovemaking.

'There'll be times I have to go back to Aristo—for family reasons—but they'll be visits. Short trips, Holly, and you'll be at my side. As my wife. With no clipped wings, either. You're not my captive wife, my love. You're my heart, my family, my world.'

She listened now to the echoes of the words held in her heart all this night, and she knew his words would stay with her until the end.

But still this unease.

She stirred and he let her go, reluctantly, waking and smiling as she wound a sheet self-consciously round her nakedness and headed for the kitchen where the pile of groceries that had arrived the day before lay yet unpacked. It had been too big a day for Honey to find time to unpack the non-perishables.

Where…?

Ten minutes later she was back. Andreas was still awake, watching for her. He held out his arms to welcome her, but she shook her head.

'Andreas, I have something… I have somewhere we need to be. Will you come with me?'

He didn't question her or protest. Silently they slipped on jeans, shirts and boots. Deefer didn't stir. It had been a big day for one small puppy, and he graciously let them go to the big outside without him.

Holly didn't speak even as they left the house. Her heart seemed too full for speech. She took his hand and silently led her love down through the home paddock, to the ancient gum where her Adam lay.

She paused at the grave. Andreas looked at her for a long moment in the moonlight, searching her face—and then he stooped before the grave.

He ran his hands through the soft leaf litter, and then he traced the wording on the gravestone with one gentle finger. The moon was full. Holly could read the inscription plainly as Andreas traced the words.

Adam Andreas Cavanagh. Her baby, loved with all her heart.

'My son,' Andreas whispered at last, and there was a world of regret in his voice. He looked up at Holly and she knelt with him, her hand resting over his on the gravestone.

'Adam was a blessing,' she whispered. 'A joy. Tomorrow I'll show you photographs. He looked just like his daddy.'

'I so wish…'

'Hush,' she whispered and she tugged his face to hers and kissed him tenderly. The grief she'd felt for all these long years was in his face now. A grief shared.

But it was right to share this grief. Adam had his father, here now to help tend his grave. And in the future…

'Andreas, do you remember, years ago when we made love? Do you remember that we took precautions?'

'They obviously didn't work,' Andreas said wryly.

'No. They didn't.'

Something in her voice gave him pause. He drew back, his brow snapping down into a question, searching her face. Stunned.

'Uh huh,' she said—and she managed a wavering smile. The emotions within her were almost too strong for smiles.

'What…are you saying…?'

'I'm saying we proved once we make a fiery couple,' she whispered. 'We're a match for any condom, it seems. Us and our kids.'

'Our kids.'

'We've lost Adam,' she whispered and her fingers traced the contours of grief still etched on his face. 'But he's with us still, in our hearts. And in eight months' time…'

'You're pregnant,' he whispered. 'You're pregnant!'

There was no mistaking his reaction. It was said with a hushed, whispered awe. Joy flooded his face, light after dark. 'You're having our baby?'

'I didn't know how to tell you,' she whispered. 'I wasn't sure. I was just starting to suspect. But we had a load of groceries come in with the road-train today and I sort of happened to put a testing kit on the end of the order.'

'So it's confirmed?'

'It's confirmed,' she said and smiled properly this time and waited for him to take her in his arms.

But he didn't. It was almost as if he had too much joy to take in. Slowly he turned again to the tiny grave. He touched the headstone again, with such tenderness that Holly was awed herself.

'I wasn't here for your mother when you both needed me,'

he said softly, tenderly. 'I swear I'll be here for her from this day on. And you, my son… You'll be a part of our family for ever.'

It was enough. She was weeping, smiling through tears, not caring that tears she'd always thought of as weakness were slipping down her face and there was no way she could stop them. She could see the glimmer of tears in Andreas's eyes as well.

We're a couple of cry-babies, she thought.

But then Andreas smiled at her and took her into his arms and held her against him. This was no cry-baby. This was her prince. Her man.

'My family,' he whispered. 'My lovely, captive bride, captive no more. It's me who's the captive now. Captured by love. For ever.'

He tugged her back into the soft bed of leaf litter. He kissed her tenderly and he told her the things that were in his heart.

And later, back in the warmth of the house, he loved her all through the night, and into the dawn—and into the rest of their lives.

* * * * *

About the Author

Marion Lennox was raised in a farming community in practically the only part of Australia that's wet all year round. With no entertainment but reading and no one to talk to but cows, it's no wonder she turned to writing. But they didn't put romance writer in the career handbook at her local school, so she pursued something she thought might make her a better living.

Marion ended up teaching statistics and computing at her local university. She married, she had a couple of kids, she acquired dogs, cats, chooks, goldfish—the full domestic catastrophe—but her first love was always romance. She penned her first novel while on family leave with her second child. *Dare To Love Again* was published in 1990 and stands as a testament to a family's ability to survive on spaghetti and toasted sandwiches.

Marion has now written more than fifty romance novels. For a while she wrote under the pseudonym Trisha David to separate her Tender Romance novels from her Medical Romance novels, so if you're looking for older books try Trisha.

She's given up teaching. She's trying to give up housework—if only the animals would stop molting and the kids would learn to clean up. (So…she's a dreamer.) She daydreams in the garden and calls it gardening. She daydreams while traveling and calls it research.

She indulges in her first love, romance.

*Turn the page for our exclusive interview
with Marion Lennox!*

We chatted to Marion Lennox about the world of THE ROYAL HOUSE OF KAREDES. *Here are her insights!*

Would you prefer to live on Aristo or Calista? What appeals to you most about either island?

They're both fabulous islands and I can't decide—so I solved the dilemma by creating another. My hero, Prince Andreas from Aristo, has been given his own smaller island by the old king. It's his private retreat and it takes the best of both islands—he's built a magnificent Bedouin-style pavilion in a coastal paradise, and it's all his own. Though he's willing to share—once he finds the right woman.

What did you enjoy about writing about the Royal House of Karedes?

The sheer opulence, the fantasy world of royalty, setting, intrigue... I read the synopses for the whole series and wanted to write them all!

How did you find writing part of a continuity?

I loved the pooling of imagination, the combined fantasy of so many talented authors and editors and the fun as we created our very own world. The book seemed to almost write itself.

When you are writing, what is your typical day?

Ooh, this is where fantasy stops. I'd love to say I lie back on my chaise lounge between the hours of two and maybe three-thirty on a hard day, I sip my champagne, I cuddle my poodle and I dictate a chapter or two to my dedicated secretaries.

The reality is I put my butt on chair at 9:00 a.m. and keep

going until I've written two thousand words. I do have a dog, who requires me to open the windows and doors every so often, but where's a good secretary when you need them? And I don't even think about champagne.

Where do you get your inspiration for the characters you write?

I'm always on the lookout for my gorgeous characters. I try hard not to use Johnny Depp as inspiration all the time, but he's pretty compelling. I generally do a collage so there are pictures in front of me as I write. For my book in progress I have an old picture of Paul Newman—mmmmmm.

What did you like most about your hero and heroine in this continuity?

They're both so torn between what they know to be right and their almost irresistible attraction to each other. If I had to describe either of them I'd say they were morally magnificent—and sexy enough to curl your toes.

What would be the best and the worst thing about being part of a royal dynasty?

The best? Ooh, I'd have to say the bling. The sheer, over-the-top fantasy. Plus having your very own hairdresser on hand every morning. (Okay, this is my own personal little fantasy—it was the only thing I ever really begrudged Princess Di.)

The worst? Being born into a role and not being given a choice in your direction in life. That's what my Prince Andreas is fighting.

Are diamonds really a girl's best friend?

Sorry. Best friends are a girl's best friend. Sisterhood—all power to women. Followed by a fabulous romance with the "best friend" to die for. Followed by your hairdresser (see above). Diamonds? Okay, they may be fourth on my list, but I wouldn't be knocking back a tasteful little three-carat number.

Who will reunite the Stefani Diamond and rule Adamas?
Look for the next book in the fabulous
ROYAL HOUSE OF KAREDES *series:*

THE SHEIKH'S FORBIDDEN VIRGIN
by
Kate Hewitt

Taken by the sheikh for pleasure—but as his bride...?

At her coming-of-age at twenty-one, Kalila is pledged to
marry the Calistan king. Scarred, sexy Sheikh Prince
Aarif is sent to escort her, his brother's betrothed, to
Calista. But when the willful virgin tries to escape, he has
to catch her, and the desert heat leads to scorching
desire—a desire that is forbidden!

Aarif claims Kalila's virginity—even though she can
never be his! Once she comes to walk up the aisle on the
day of her wedding, Kalila's heart is in her mouth: *who
is waiting to become her husband at the altar?*

Turn the page for an exclusive extract!

A LIGHT, INQUIRING KNOCK SOUNDED on the door, and, turning from that grim reminder, Aarif left the bathroom and went to fulfill his brother's bidding, and express his greetings to his bride.

The official led him to the double doors of the Throne Room; inside, an expectant hush fell like a curtain being dropped into place, or perhaps pulled up.

"Your Eminence," the official said in French, the national language of Zaraq, his voice low and unctuous, "may I present His Royal Highness, King Zakari."

Aarif choked; the sound was lost amid a ripple of murmurings from the palace staff, who had assembled for this honored occasion. It would take King Bahir only one glance to realize it was not the king who graced his Throne Room today, but rather the king's brother, a lowly prince.

Aarif felt a flash of rage—directed at himself. A mistake had been made in the correspondence, he supposed. He'd delegated the task to an aide when he should have written himself and explained that he would be coming rather than his brother.

Now he would have to explain the mishap in front of company—all of Bahir's staff—and he feared the insult could be great.

"Your Eminence," he said, also speaking French, and moved into the long, narrow room with its frescoed ceilings and bare walls. He bowed, not out of obeisance but rather respect, and heard Bahir shift in his chair. "I fear my brother, His Royal Highness Zakari, was unable to attend to this glad errand, due to pressing royal business. I am honored to escort his bride, the princess Kalila, to Calista in his stead."

Bahir was silent, and, stifling a prickle of both alarm and irritation, Aarif rose. He was conscious of Bahir watching him, his skin smooth but his eyes shrewd, his mouth tightening with disappointment or displeasure, perhaps both.

Yet even before Bahir made a reply, even before the formalities had been dispensed with, Aarif found his gaze sliding, of its own accord, to the silent figure to Bahir's right.

It was his daughter, of course. Kalila. Aarif had a memory of a pretty, precocious child. He'd spoken a few words to her at the engagement party more than ten years ago now. Yet now the woman standing before him was lovely, although, he acknowledged wryly, he could see little of her.

Her head was bowed, her figure swathed in a kaftan, and yet, as if she felt the magnetic tug of his gaze, she lifted her head and her eyes met his.

It was all he could see of her, those eyes; they were almond-shaped, wide and dark, luxuriously fringed, a deep, clear golden brown. Every emotion could be seen in them, including the one that flickered there now as her gaze was drawn inexorably to his face, to his scar.

It was disgust Aarif thought he saw flare in their golden depths, and as their gazes held and clashed he felt a sharp, answering stab of disappointment and self-loathing in his own gut.

* * * * *

Be sure to look for
THE SHEIKH'S FORBIDDEN VIRGIN
by Kate Hewitt,
available October from Harlequin Presents®!

HARLEQUIN *Presents*

TWO CROWNS, TWO ISLANDS, ONE LEGACY

A royal family torn apart by pride and its lust for power, reunited by purity and passion

THE ROYAL HOUSE *of* KAREDES

Look for the next passionate adventure in
The Royal House of Karedes:

THE SHEIKH'S FORBIDDEN VIRGIN
by Kate Hewitt, October 2009

THE GREEK BILLIONAIRE'S INNOCENT PRINCESS
by Chantelle Shaw, November 2009

THE FUTURE KING'S LOVE-CHILD
by Melanie Milburne, December 2009

RUTHLESS BOSS, ROYAL MISTRESS
by Natalie Anderson, January 2010

THE DESERT KING'S HOUSEKEEPER BRIDE
by Carol Marinelli, February 2010

REQUEST YOUR FREE BOOKS!

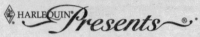

2 FREE NOVELS
PLUS 2
FREE GIFTS!

PASSION **GUARANTEED** SEDUCTION

YES! Please send me 2 FREE Harlequin Presents® novels and my 2 FREE gifts (gifts are worth about $10). After receiving them, if I don't wish to receive any more books, I can return the shipping statement marked "cancel". If I don't cancel, I will receive 6 brand-new novels every month and be billed just $4.05 per book in the U.S. or $4.74 per book in Canada. That's a savings of close to 15% off the cover price! It's quite a bargain! Shipping and handling is just 50¢ per book*. I understand that accepting the 2 free books and gifts places me under no obligation to buy anything. I can always return a shipment and cancel at any time. Even if I never buy another book, the two free books and gifts are mine to keep forever.

106 HDN EYRQ 306 HDN EYR2

Name _____ (PLEASE PRINT)

Address _____ Apt. #

City _____ State/Prov. _____ Zip/Postal Code

Signature (if under 18, a parent or guardian must sign)

Mail to the **Harlequin Reader Service:**
IN U.S.A.: P.O. Box 1867, Buffalo, NY 14240-1867
IN CANADA: P.O. Box 609, Fort Erie, Ontario L2A 5X3

Not valid to current subscribers of Harlequin Presents books.

Are you a current subscriber of Harlequin Presents books and want to receive the larger-print edition? Call 1-800-873-8635 today!

* Terms and prices subject to change without notice. Prices do not include applicable taxes. Sales tax applicable in N.Y. Canadian residents will be charged applicable provincial taxes and GST. Offer not valid in Quebec. This offer is limited to one order per household. All orders subject to approval. Credit or debit balances in a customer's account(s) may be offset by any other outstanding balance owed by or to the customer. Please allow 4 to 6 weeks for delivery. Offer available while quantities last.

Your Privacy: Harlequin Books is committed to protecting your privacy. Our Privacy Policy is available online at www.eHarlequin.com or upon request from the Reader Service. From time to time we make our lists of customers available to reputable third parties who may have a product or service of interest to you. If you would prefer we not share your name and address, please check here. ☐

HP09R

You're invited to join our Tell Harlequin Reader Panel!

By joining our new reader panel you will:

- Receive Harlequin® books—they are FREE and yours to keep with no obligation to purchase anything!
- Participate in fun online surveys
- Exchange opinions and ideas with women just like you
- Have a say in our new book ideas and help us publish the best in women's fiction

In addition, you will have a chance to win great prizes and receive special gifts! See Web site for details. Some conditions apply. Space is limited.

To join, visit us at
www.TellHarlequin.com.

Stay up-to-date on all your romance reading news!

The Harlequin Inside Romance newsletter is a **FREE** quarterly newsletter highlighting our upcoming series releases and promotions!

Go to
eHarlequin.com/InsideRomance
or e-mail us at
InsideRomance@Harlequin.com
to sign up to receive
your **FREE** newsletter today!

You can also subscribe by writing to us at: HARLEQUIN BOOKS
Attention: Customer Service Department
P.O. Box 9057, Buffalo, NY 14269-9057

Please allow 4-6 weeks for delivery of the first issue by mail.

IRNBPAQ209

I ♥ HARLEQUIN *Presents*

BROUGHT TO YOU BY FANS OF
HARLEQUIN PRESENTS.

We are its editors and authors
and biggest fans—and we'd
love to hear from YOU!

Subscribe today to our online blog at
www.iheartpresents.com